KEN PR KU-060-427

THE LOST CITY

Complete and Unabridged

LINFORD
Leicester

First published in Great Britain in 2020

First Linford Edition
published 2021

Copyright © 2020 by DC Thomson & Co. Ltd.,
and Ken Preston
All rights reserved

A catalogue record for this book is available
from the British Library.

ISBN 978–1–4448–4807–6

Published by
Ulverscroft Limited
Anstey, Leicestershire

Printed and bound in Great Britain by
TJ Books Ltd., Padstow, Cornwall

This book is printed on acid-free paper

THE LOST CITY

It was supposed to be the happiest day of Kirstin's life! A lavish wedding to fellow adventurer Charles, with her friends and family — including teenage daughter Naomi — all present. What could possibly go wrong? And how could events then conspire to leave Kirstin and Naomi — along with the handsome pilot Josh — in the middle of the Amazonian jungle, on a dangerous quest for the mythical Lost City of Quetzalcoatl?

1

The chime of the bell rang out clear and loud across the Palazzo. One strike and then, a moment later, a second one. The young man in charge of the gondola, wearing the typical striped vest, reached out his hand. Kirstin took it and used her other hand to gather up the folds of her wedding dress. It seemed as though a dozen or more young men appeared out of nowhere to help her with her train and keep it from trailing into the canal's water.

The stunning architecture of the Basilica San Marco sparkled in the sunlight. Tourists wandering across the piazza stopped and gazed at Kirstin and smiled. Someone, Kirstin wasn't sure who, handed her bouquet over, and she held it in front of her. Mr Dewberry's PA trotted up to Kirstin and began fussing with the wedding dress, pinching it here, fluffing it up there. Finally she reached up and slowly pulled the veil down and adjusted it over Kirstin's face.

She stood back and assessed her work.

'So beautiful!' She pulled out a white handkerchief and dabbed at her eyes. The photographer elbowed the PA out of his way and snapped off a series of photos.

Kirstin felt a hand on her arm and turned to see her father, his face a picture of pride and love.

'You look absolutely stunning,' he said.

'Thank you,' Kirstin said, smiling. 'Where is Naomi?'

Her father chuckled and said, 'Over there.'

Kirstin's daughter strolled towards them. Thirteen years old and she was turning into a beautiful young woman. Kirstin blinked as tears of love gathered behind her eyelids.

A sudden cry from the crowd that had gathered to watch the wedding procession had Kirstin turning to see a flock of white doves scattering from the square and up into the sky. 'Did Charles arrange that?' Kirstin's father said.

Kirstin's jaw ached from the grin stretched across her face. 'I have no idea, but I wouldn't put it past him.'

They stood in silence and watched the doves fly away, disappearing behind the towers of the Basilica San Marco where, very soon, Kirstin would become Mrs Dewberry.

On her left, Kirstin linked arms with her father, and on her right with Naomi.

'Shall we . . . ? Oh, Naomi, what's the matter?'

Naomi bit her bottom lip, and her frown deepened. 'I'm so sorry Mum, I want to be happy for you, I really do.'

Kirstin sighed. 'I know. Can you, maybe, just pretend?'

Naomi lowered her head and looked at the ground. Then she looked up, gave her mother a forced smile, and nodded.

Kirstin smiled back. 'Thank you.'

They began the procession across the square to the church. Quite a crowd had gathered now, and it parted to form a path towards the massive church doors. Kirstin glanced back and saw the crowd closing in behind them, and more people lining the bridges across the canal. From deep inside the church echoed the sonorous notes of the organ.

This was the fairytale wedding every girl ever wanted. And it was Kirstin's.

If only Naomi could be happy for her. The last few years had been hard, but this was the start of a new chapter for them both. Naomi would grow to love Charles, eventually. Kirstin was sure that the speed with which the courtship and the marriage proposal had happened were a factor in Naomi's unhappiness. That and perhaps Charles's wealth, which was something Kirstin was still having to become used to.

Once the wedding celebration was over and Naomi was back in England with her grandparents, perhaps then she could have some time to grow used to the idea. And when Kirstin and Charles returned from honeymoon, back in their positions at the university and normal, everyday life, Naomi would be forced to the conclusion that this was how things were going to be from now on.

Charles was now a part of their lives, whether or not Naomi was happy about it.

Two ushers stood either side of the entrance to the church. They were friends of Charles, and Kirstin hardly knew them. They smiled and nodded encouragement. Then they both approached, and each gave her a kiss on the cheek.

Tarquin (was that his name?) grinned and shook his head. 'I'm afraid that your taste in men is poor, but Charles's taste in women is superb.'

Kirstin slapped him playfully. 'Stop it, now.'

They stepped into the foyer. Kirstin paused to look through the doorway at the vaulted ceilings, the marbled floor and the frescoed walls, and the expectant faces turned to look at her from the pews. Sunlight streamed through the stain glass windows, casting a warm glow over the cathedral's interior.

Kirstin's chest filled with happiness until she thought she might explode. This was perfect, so utterly, wonderfully perfect. The dream wedding.

The sunlight faded, the warm shafts of light from the windows fading away. A sudden gloom seemed to settle over the wedding guests.

Kirstin shivered as a cold breeze fluttered over her bare shoulders.

Her father glanced at her. 'Are you alright?'

Just then the sunlight began streaming through the colourful windows once more and the gloom lifted. A cloud, blocking the sun for a moment but passing on now. That was all it had been.

Kirstin smiled at her dad. 'Yes, I'm fine.'

The tall, golden pipes of the church organ fell silent for a moment before the first notes of the Wedding March began.

Kirstin glanced nervously at her father and at Naomi. Her father gave her another reassuring smile and, much to Kirstin's relief, so did Naomi.

They began the walk down the marble aisle where, standing in front of the altar, Charles waited for Kirstin.

★ ★ ★

'Oh, it was so beautiful!'

Jacqui threw her arms around Kirstin's neck and began sobbing. Kirstin giggled and embraced her sister and best friend in the whole world. 'Don't be silly, come on, don't cry.'

'I can't help it,' Jacqui sobbed, her voice muffled in Kirstin's head dress. 'You look so beautiful, and the church service was beautiful, and it's all so amazing.'

Kirstin looked over Jacqui's head at David, who simply raised his eyebrows and gave Kirstin an uncomfortable smile. That was typical of Jacqui's husband, who never seemed quite sure where he was or what he was there for. Behind him snaked the line of wedding guests still waiting to greet the bride and groom.

'Come on now, pull yourself together,' Charles said, laughing as he patted

Jacqui on the back.

Jacqui suddenly pulled away from Kirstin and wiped at her red and puffy eyes with the heel of her hand. Stabbing a finger in Charles's chest, Jacqui said, 'Now you make sure you look after her, or you'll have me to answer to.'

David looked down at his feet as he muttered something. Kirstin had to stop herself from laughing out loud. David was always complaining about being hen-pecked.

Charles, looking amazing in his suit, held up his hands in surrender. 'I promise, I promise!'

'You'd better,' Jacqui said, before giving Kirstin another hug. 'Come on, David, you're holding up the wedding line.'

The line of guests, many of whom Kirstin had never met before, seemed endless. The words she repeated, (*Hello, how are you? Thank you so much for coming. Yes, it was beautiful, wasn't it?*) became automatic for Kirstin, and her mind began to wander. How much had this all cost? Never in her wildest dreams could

Kirstin have imagined marrying like this, in such splendour and opulence. How rich was Charles's family, that they could afford this?

'Congratulations, Kirstin.'

The cold, flat voice shocked Kirstin out of her thoughts and back to the moment. Julia, Kirstin's cousin from her father's side of the family, held out her hand for Kirstin to shake. Typical of her, that she wouldn't offer an embrace, that she limited physical contact to the bare minimum. Her long, straight dark hair framed her pale face, accentuating her high cheekbones and large, round eyes. The tight dress she wore perfectly displayed her slim figure and long legs. And the tattoo of a skull and crossbones on her right shoulder. Julia always drew stares wherever she went, and today was no different. Kirstin had to force back a surge of jealousy that Julia was stealing attention away from her special day.

By Julia's side stood her son, who was just a couple of years younger than Naomi. Tyler was good looking and, according to Naomi, 'the coolest boy in the universe', but Kirstin wasn't sure how much she liked him. Was that simply because she disliked Julia? And besides, the poor boy didn't spend all that much time with his mother as she loved partying so often.

'Thank you.' Kirstin took Julia's hand and gave it a brief shake. 'Did you enjoy the ceremony?'

Julia's red lips parted in what Kirstin could only imagine was meant to be a smile. 'Beautiful, of course, just like you.'

'Isn't she just?' Charles said.

'Charles, this is my cousin, Julia.'

Charles bowed a little, and he gave her a smile. 'I'm very pleased to meet you. Now, how come Kirstin has never introduced us before?'

Julia took his hand to shake, and was it Kirstin's imagination or did Julia's touch linger a little too long?

'Julia and Tyler have only recently returned to the UK after a year or two away,' Kirstin said. 'You've been travelling, haven't you?'

10

'Oh yes, all over,' Julia said, keeping her gaze on Charles.

'Sounds fascinating,' Charles purred. 'You must tell me more.'

Kirstin dragged her eyes away from her cousin and new husband as another guest in the never-ending line of guests began talking to her. Despite trying her best to concentrate on what was being said, Kirstin couldn't stop thinking about Charles and Julia. Kirstin had no idea where Julia and Tyler had been for the last two years.

Julia had arrived back in the UK unannounced and immediately managed to wrangle an invitation to the wedding. Kirstin hadn't wanted her here, but Charles was paying and he had said it seemed unfair to invite the rest of the family without Julia. Kirstin risked a quick glance at her new husband and saw that Julia had moved on. Charles gave Kirstin a reassuring smile.

Finally, the never-ending line of guests actually came to an end. Kirstin and Charles circulated among the guests whilst champagne and canapes were dispensed by the serving staff. Kirstin slowly but surely made her way towards her mother and father, sitting with her grandfather who had been confined to his wheelchair for the last year.

Kirstin bent down and gave him a loving hug.

'You look beautiful, Dora,' Walter said. Dora was his nickname for Kirstin, given to her as a child when she had been obsessed with the cartoon show *Dora the Explorer*. Kirstin sat down next to him. 'Look at you in your suit. I never realised you scrubbed up this nice.'

Walter laughed quietly. At ninety-six years old, his mind was still sharp. He took her hand and gave it a gentle squeeze. 'I was thinking exactly the same about you. This makes a change from tramping through a muddy field on a cold and wet November, doesn't it?'

Kirstin leaned in close and whispered, 'I know where I would rather be.'

Walter laughed and patted her hand. 'Don't be silly. There's plenty of time yet for that.'

Not with you, though, Kirstin thought, sadly. Long gone were the days when Kirstin and her grandfather had spent weekends exploring, or visiting archaeological sites. It was because of Walter and his passion for archaeology that Kirstin had grown up with her own fierce love of the ancient past.

The rest of the day passed in a flurry of food, (twelve courses), endlessly flowing rivers of alcohol (champagne and wine), wedding cake, (eight tiers) and speeches.

'Of course, Kirstin would fall in love with a man who shared her passion for looking for things,' Kirstin's father said in his speech. 'Ancient things, not just the TV remote stuffed down the back of the settee. No, my daughter enjoys looking for ancient, long lost cities. You'd think it would be fairly easy to find a city, wouldn't you? But apparently not. Kirstin has dedicated the last ten years of her life searching for the lost city of Quetzalcoatl and, it turns out, so has Charles.

That's what brought them together. Have either of you had any luck finding it yet?'

Charles shook his head, a rueful grin on his face.

'I think we lost it down the back of the settee!' Kirstin laughed.

The room full of guests laughed with her.

Her father nodded and smiled gently. 'That's right, you haven't found your lost city yet. But now, with the two of you working together, I don't think it will be long before you find that city. And I know that will be an amazing day, a day to celebrate. But it will still be nothing compared to today.'

Kirstin looked up at her father, and he gazed back at her. He raised his glass. The wedding guests stood up and raised their glasses too.

'May your love for each other grow with the passing of the days and years, and at the end of all your rainbows may you find not a pot of gold, but a lost city or two.'

A ripple of laughter coursed through the great hall. 'To the bride and groom!'

* * *

As the special day wore on and the sun began to set over the Venetian canals, lights sprang on in the vast reception hall and the evening meal was brought out.

Kirstin glanced around the vast hall, looking for Naomi. It seemed like hours since she had last seen her. Kirstin knew that this day would have been a tough one for her daughter, especially coming on top of the problems she was having at school. But Naomi would just have to accept that her mother was married now, that Naomi had a step-father, and she had to learn to love him. Or, if she couldn't love him, at least put up with him.

Kirstin wandered through the hall looking for Naomi. She found her parents relaxing on a sofa in another room with her grandfather. 'Have you seen Naomi?'

'She said she was heading up to her room for a lie down,' Kirstin's mother replied.

Kirstin walked out to the lobby and up the stairs. Her feet had begun to ache, so she slipped off her shoes and carried them as she climbed the carpeted steps. There was probably nothing to worry about, Naomi would have simply wanted some time to herself. Too much time spent around others seemed to wear her out emotionally. But still, Kirstin knew she would feel better once she had checked on her daughter.

Kirstin padded softly down the hall and paused at the door to hers and Charles's room. Was that a giggle she had just heard from inside? And then she realised she hadn't seen Charles for a little while either.

A soft glow of warmth radiated through Kirstin's chest as she realised what must have happened. Charles had seen how difficult Naomi was finding the day and had escorted her upstairs for some rest. And he had stayed behind a little to get to know her better, to try and break down the wall of reserve that Naomi had thrown up between them.

And it sounded like it was working.

Kirstin pulled her room pass from her bag and tapped it against the door's lock. The green light sprang on to indicate the door was now unlocked.

Kirstin pushed open the door and stepped inside her room.

The first thing she noticed were the clothes strewn across the floor.

Then she saw Charles and Julia as they turned to look at her, their eyes wide.

'Oh!' Kirstin gasped.

2

Six months later

Beads of sweat ran down Kirstin's face and into her eyes. She blinked and pushed her long, dark hair off her face. Joshua Hanson pulled his hat a little lower over his face to shield his eyes from the sun. 'Like I said, nobody's going anywhere for the next twenty-four hours at least. That breeze you can feel is just going to get stronger and stronger until it turns into a storm.'

Hanson wore tan fatigues, his shirt-sleeves rolled up to his elbows, and his hands were black with engine oil. Standing by his plane, the engine exposed where he had been working on it, Hanson looked the part of a world-weary adventurer who'd just about had enough of other people.

Kirstin knew how he felt.

'You don't understand, Mr Hanson, we need to leave now,' Kirstin said. 'I appreciate what you're telling me about the weather conditions, but we don't need to go far and we could be back on the ground before the wind really starts to pick up.'

'Is that right?' Hanson wiped at his hands with a filthy rag. 'And where exactly do you intend on coming back down to ground? The nearest airstrip is over a hundred miles south of here. We'd be flying right into the storm.'

'I don't need to land at an airstrip, we can land anywhere.' Kirstin tried to keep the panic out of her voice. 'We just need to get away from here.'

Hanson grinned and shook his head. 'Listen to me, lady, we can't just land anywhere we like out there. Not only do I have to find a space where we can land safely, but I have to make sure we can get back up in the air again. If the spot we touch down on is too soft, or it's not level, if there isn't a long enough run up to get us in the air again, well that's it. We're stranded. This is the Amazon, not JFK airport.'

Kirstin glanced over her shoulder. The single dirt track road led away from the tiny airport and crawled along the coastline in a long, curved loop until it disappeared behind a bay in the distance. Apart from Kirstin's jeep just visible in the distance, the road was empty of people and trucks. The jeep's engine had been struggling since she started it up earlier that morning, until it had finally given up with a grunt and a cloud of black smoke. Kirstin had spotted the tiny airport, and they had walked the rest of the way.

Yes, the road was empty, but it wouldn't be that way for much longer.

She turned to look at Hanson again and made an effort to put on her best smile. 'Mr Hanson, you're a professional, and if you think it's not safe to go south, I'm happy to go north instead.'

'North!' Hanson burst out laughing. 'There's nothing north for over a thousand miles, except the river and the forest.'

'That is so gross!' Naomi stepped out

of the wooden shack that served as an office for Hanson, shaking water off her hands. 'Doesn't anybody clean the toilet out here?'

Hanson rolled his eyes. 'I don't usually have visitors, and when I do, they're not that picky about bathroom hygiene.'

Kirstin looked over her shoulder again. Still nothing. Thankfully. But they would be here soon, she was sure of that.

Kirstin turned her attention back to Hanson. 'Please, just take us anywhere you like, north, south, I don't care, anywhere on the compass I really don't care. We just need to leave right now.'

Hanson stood up a little straighter and narrowed his eyes, shaded by the brim of his hat. 'What's the big rush? Are you in some kind of trouble?'

That was the question, wasn't it? Yes, she was in trouble, big trouble, but trying to explain what kind of trouble, and convince this man of the truth of it, was going to take far too long.

Kirstin glanced over her shoulder again. And this time she saw it. The truck, fuzzy and indistinct in the distance and so small it looked like a toy, racing along the coastline towards them.

Kirstin rounded on Hanson. 'We have to go now! See that truck back there? It is full of bad men with guns. And they will shoot us all unless you get us out of here, right now!'

'Mum?' Naomi said.

Kirstin beckoned her closer and hugged her tight. 'It's going to be alright.'

Hanson dropped the rag and stared into the distance. 'Are you sure about this?'

Kirstin nodded.

Hanson continued staring at the tiny truck on the horizon, his eyes narrowed down to slits in the bright sunlight. 'Who are those people?'

The truck had stopped and a group of tiny figures had jumped out and were examining Kirstin's broken down jeep.

Kirstin didn't answer. Instead, she picked up her rucksack and slung it over her shoulder. She grabbed Naomi's smaller bag and threw it to her.

Hanson, his back to Kirstin and Naomi, was still staring into the distance. The men had climbed back into their truck. A cloud of dust kicked up as the truck began racing towards them once more.

'Please, we don't have time to stand around and wait!' Kirstin pleaded.

Hanson turned around. 'Hey! What do you think you're doing?'

Kirstin paused by the plane. She had been about to climb into the cockpit with her rucksack.

'Aren't we going? We need to leave now.'

'Look, lady, I don't know who those people are, but I'm not taking Janice up without a good — '

'Janice? Who's Janice?' Naomi said.

Hanson pointed at the plane. 'You're looking at her.'

'You called your plane Janice?'

'Yeah, what's wrong with that?'

'Can we talk about this later?' Kirstin yelled.

Hanson shook his head. 'Look, you

don't seem to understand, so let me put this in words of one syllable. I am not flying —'

'That's two syllables,' Naomi said.

'Don't be smart, kid,' Hanson snapped, and turned back to Kirstin. 'We are not going up in the air today. Whoever those guys are, I'm going to talk to them and whatever trouble you're in, we're going to smooth it all out, okay?'

A window in Hanson's office shattered in an explosion of glass. 'I don't believe it!' Hanson yelled, spinning around to look at the approaching truck. 'They're shooting at us!'

'I told you!' Kirstin shouted and climbed onto the wing of the plane.

'Careful where you put your feet!' Hanson said, running to the plane. He slammed the engine bonnet shut and then helped Naomi climb into the cabin. Another window shattered in Hanson's office, and a small cloud of sand kicked up on the ground. Hanson climbed into the pilot's seat next to Kirstin and closed the cover.

He started the engine. A cloud of dark purple smoke billowed past them as the engine sputtered into life. 'Will this thing even get off the ground?' Kirstin said.

Hanson tapped at a dial on the dashboard, and the needle sprang from zero to full. 'Janice always gets off the ground, don't you girl?'

'Mum?' Naomi said from the back. 'They're getting close.'

Kirstin glanced out of her window. The beaten up old truck seemed much larger now. Its wheels kicked up plumes of dirt behind it and the canvas covering and the cab were caked with a thick layer of filth. It was so close now that Kirstin could even pick out the man leaning out of the passenger side of the cab and pointing a gun. And she could hear the crack of the gun as the man shot at the plane.

'You seriously managed to annoy them, didn't you?' Hanson said as he angled the plane to point down the runway.

The note of the engine picked up as they increased speed. The plane bumped along the uneven runway, rattling Kirstin's teeth together.

'Hold on!' Kirstin shouted to Naomi. 'I think this rust-bucket might fall apart before we even get off the ground!'

'Rust-bucket?' Hanson turned his head and scowled at Kirstin. 'This rust-bucket is about to save us from getting shot.'

'I'll believe it when I see it,' Kirstin muttered.

And then, for one exhilarating moment, they left the ground, and they were airborne.

Kirstin almost shrieked with delight, but they were back on the ground, bumping along the runway, before she had a chance.

'Come on Janice, don't let me down,' Hanson muttered, as he fought with the controls.

The plane was shaking so much that Katrina could hardly see straight.

'Aren't runways meant to be flat and smooth?' she shouted.

'What runway?' Hanson shouted back.

'I told you, this is the Amazon, not JFK.'

Kirstin closed her eyes. They were going to die.

Just as that thought entered her mind, and as despair began to wash over her, the plane magically lifted from the ground once more.

And this time they stayed airborne.

Kirstin opened her eyes and looked out of her window as Hanson pulled them up in a steep climb. They had taken off just in time. The truck had skidded to a halt below them and men were leaning out of the cab and firing at the plane.

Hanson banked the plane and Kirstin lost sight of the men on the ground.

Hanson levelled the plane and let out a long sigh. 'That was a close one.'

Kirstin had to agree. That had been too close.

She craned her head back.

'Are you alright?' she said.

Naomi nodded. She looked a little pale, a little shocked, but she was alright.

Kirstin twisted back around to face forward. Up ahead, the sky was growing darker.

'Okay, now I got us up in the air and away from those trigger happy goons back there, you can do something for me,' Hanson said.

'Like what?'

Hanson looked her in the eye. 'Like tell me just what on earth is going on here?'

Kirstin nodded. She supposed she owed him an explanation.

The only problem was, where should she start?

3

So, where did it all start? With Charles, perhaps? Yes, that was probably the best place to begin. The day she married Charles Attlee Tarkington-Pit Cecil Dewberry.

'Hold on!' Hanson looked at Kirstin, his eyes alive with amusement. 'What on earth kind of name is that?'

'He came from landed gentry,' Kirstin said.

'Landed gentry. Okay, so does that mean he was rich?'

'Spectacularly,' Kirstin said.

'And what about you, are you rich too?'

'Of course, that's why I am here with you in a plane held together with sealing wax and spit.'

Hanson sighed. 'You really do have a way about you, don't you? Some people would be grateful that I saved them from certain death at the hands of a gang of gun-toting outlaws.'

'Gun-toting?' Naomi called from the back, having to raise her voice over the rumble of the engine. 'Are you a cowboy or something?'

Hanson twisted in his seat. 'How old are you?'

Naomi looked at him, her eyes betraying a sudden uncertainty. 'Thirteen, what's it to you?'

'Thirteen, huh? You know something? Even for a teenager you've got one bad attitude, kid.' Hanson twisted forward again.

'I apologise,' Kirstin said. 'I apologise for my daughter's attitude and for being rude about Janice. Now, do you want to hear my story?'

'Yeah, go ahead.' Hanson checked his instrument panel. 'We've got a way to go yet, we need something to pass the time.'

Kirstin continued with her story. At the sight of her cousin and brand-new husband locked in an embrace on the double bed, (thankfully they were beneath the covers), Kirstin had turned

30

on her heel and left. She had intended to slam the door shut, but at the last moment decided to leave it wide open. Let them scramble out of bed and shut the door. Hopefully a wedding guest or two would be walking past at that exact moment.

Kirstin stalked down the hall to Naomi's room and banged her fist on the door.

'Who is it?'

'It's your mum, let me in.'

Naomi opened the door, her face a picture of apprehension. 'What's wrong?'

'Pack your bag, we're going home.'

A voice echoed down the hall. 'Kirstin!'

'Is that Charles?' Naomi said.

Kirstin pushed the door wider and stepped inside Naomi's room. She shoved the door shut just as Charles arrived and knocked on it.

'Let me in!' he shouted.

'You were right,' Kirstin said, gazing at her daughter. 'I should have listened to you, and I'm sorry I didn't. Charles is not going to be my husband after all.'

Naomi's eyes filled with tears. 'Oh Mum, no, I'm sorry.'

The next few hours were burned into Kirstin's mind as the most hideous few hours of her life. As much as she was desperate to stay away from Charles and Julia, she had to go back to her room and collect her belongings. And there were the guests to face, and her parents. The confusion, the anger, the recriminations and the shame.

Most of all, the shame.

Kirstin got on the telephone and, after an hour of pleading and cajoling, managed to book a flight back to the UK later that night. It meant connecting flights via Germany, Austria and France, but Kirstin didn't care.

She just had to get away.

And it was ridiculous, wasn't it? Kirstin was the victim here, the one who had been cheated on. And yet she felt such a burning sense of shame that she could hardly look her guests in the eye. Particularly her parents. It seemed Naomi was the only one she could trust, the only one she could depend upon to fully understand what she was going through.

Back in England, Kirstin girded herself for the start of a new term at the university. Kirstin and Charles were both lecturers in archaeology, it was where they had met. Despite never wanting to see that man again, Kirstin was not about to allow him to force her out of a job she loved.

The months passed in frosty silences whenever they encountered one another at the university. Charles didn't need the money, and so Kirstin wished he would simply leave. But it seemed he derived a sadistic pleasure from taunting her with his presence every day. Then came the news that Julia and Charles were to be married.

Kirstin began to think that maybe she should leave after all. But then something happened that changed everything. Her grandfather died. Walter had just celebrated his ninety-seventh birthday the week before. And then he had simply and peacefully slipped away during the night while he slept. No-one could deny that his life had been long and wonderful, that he had crammed every experience he could into almost a century of living, and that he had been warm, kind and generous. Kirstin had been realistic in her view that his time left had been limited.

But still, she missed him dreadfully.

After the funeral, Kirstin's parents decided the time had come to clear out his house. Despite his age and his reliance on a wheelchair, Walter had managed to live an independent life in his own home until the end. And he had amassed a treasure trove of belongings in his lifetime.

Kirstin's father had invited her over to Walter's house one morning to show her what he had discovered. The old-fashioned sailor's chest sat in the middle of her grandfather's living room, caked in dust and old cobwebs.

'Where on earth did you find this?' Kirstin said.

'In a cubbyhole under the stairs.'

'Have you opened it?'

Her father grinned. 'No, I wanted you to be here. I remember Dad having this trunk when I was a child. As far as I can remember it holds his journals from when he explored the continents as a young man. You know he was an explorer before he became an archaeologist, don't you?'

Kirstin nodded as a bubble of excitement formed in her chest. Her grandfather had told her some stories from his days exploring, but surely there would be much she didn't know that would be revealed in his journals?

Together, daughter and father lifted the trunk's heavy lid. The stale smell of dried, aged paper tickled Kirstin's nose. The trunk was filled with books, the covers all blank apart from a gold tracery of floral designs like old wallpaper. Kirstin looked at her dad, and he simply nodded, his eyes alive with love and excitement. Kirstin picked up a book at random and opened it.

'You were right, it's a journal.' Kirstin gently turned over the pages filled with Walter's neat, elegant handwriting.

She placed that one on the floor and picked out another. It was the same, another journal.

Her dad chuckled. 'These are going to keep you busy for a while if you intend reading them.'

'Of course I'm going to read them,' Kirstin whispered.

'This one has photographs inside,' her father said. The photos were black and white, faded and creased.

Kirstin's dad pointed at a photo of a young man looking casually into the camera. 'There he is, your granddad.'

'Oh, he's so handsome!' Kirstin gasped.

Her dad chuckled. 'Yes, he was quite the charmer I've been told.'

They turned over the page.

'Who's that?' Kirstin said, pointing to a photograph of her grandfather and another man standing together on a railway station platform, surrounded by luggage.

'That was my Uncle Edwin, your grandfather's younger brother.'

'I didn't know he had a brother!'

'Edwin went missing on an expedition, when he was a young man. Your grandfather never really liked to talk about him.'

Kirstin gazed at her father. 'But why?'

Her father looked up at Kirstin, sadness in his eyes. 'I don't know, he would never say.'

For the next few weeks she had pored over her grandfather's journals, and for a while it helped with her sadness as his words brought him back to life. And then she found his entry on The Lost City of Quetzalcoatl, the almost mythical city that explorers the world over had been in search of for the last two hundred years.

'The Lost City of Queta . . . Quilt . . . Quetaz . . . ?' Hanson said.

'The Lost City of Quetzalcoatl is an ancient city hidden deep in the Amazon rainforest. Many explorers have mounted expeditions to find it, but no-one has succeeded.'

'What's so special about this place?'

'It's a lost city, that's one reason that makes it special. The other is that there is meant to be an underground labyrinth of gold, silver and precious treasures, all used in the worship of the Aztec god, Quetzalcoatl. Quetzalcoatl was a winged serpent, the god of air and wind — '

'I like him already,' Hanson said. 'And you mentioned something about gold and precious treasures?'

'That's right,' Kirstin said. 'The Lost City of Quetzalcoatl is supposed to have the largest repository of gold and diamonds ever seen.'

Hanson started nodding. 'Okay, I see what's happening here.'

'What do you mean?'

'I mean, now I realise why you had truckloads of men with guns chasing after you. If you've got a lost city full of gold and diamonds, you're going to have every lowlife and his mother after it.'

'But I haven't told anyone!' Kirstin protested.

'So why are they after you?'

'I don't know.'

'Well, you must have done something to upset them, even if you don't know about it,' Hanson said.

'Maybe,' Kirstin said.

'Where did you first encounter them?'

'They just started following us.' Kirstin glanced back at Naomi. 'Naomi spotted them first.'

'And Mum didn't believe me!'

'Well, I just thought you were being a little neurotic. But then when we got on the trail to come down to yours, and they stopped following us and started chasing us.'

'That trail only leads one place, and that's to Hanson's Rainforest Sky Tours, so I guess they realised you were going flying and they didn't want to lose you,' Hanson said. 'Who's funding this trip?'

'Nobody.'

'Seriously?' Hanson said.

'Yeah, seriously!' Naomi said from her back seat. 'Mum's paying for all of this herself, it's her idea of a holiday.'

Kirstin shook her head. 'That's not

true. You weren't even meant to be coming with me. If you hadn't got yourself expelled from school — '

'Mum! I keep telling you, I haven't been expelled, I've been suspended!'

'Isn't it the same thing?'

Naomi appeared between Kirstin and Hanson, leaning forward. 'No, and you know it isn't.'

'What did you do to get kicked out of school?' Hanson said.

Naomi threw her head back and groaned. 'I got caught fighting with a boy.'

'Impressive.'

'Oh no, don't you go encouraging her,' Kirstin said. 'And the headmaster didn't say you were fighting, he said you were beating him up.'

'I told you, he's a bully, he had it coming.'

'And I told you, you should report things like that to your teacher.'

Naomi groaned again and flung herself back into her seat.

'Look, this is all good fun listening

to you two arguing, but I need to get you somewhere safe back down on the ground and where you can catch a flight back to the UK,' Hanson said.

'We're not going back to England,' Kirstin said. 'Not yet, not until we've found the Lost City of Quetzalcoatl.'

'Are you serious?' Hanson said. 'You're being chased by men with guns and you think that's okay? That this city of Quist . . . Qalze . . .'

'Quetzalcoatl!' Naomi shouted from the back seat of the plane.

'Yeah, whatever,' Hanson said. 'Look, all I'm trying to say is, the Amazon is no place for a woman and a teenage girl.'

'But it's alright for a man?'

Hanson gave her a lop-sided grin, and with a jolt, Kirstin realised he was actually pretty good looking. Not that it mattered. Kirstin was never allowing herself to fall for another man. Ever.

'Listen, I've been out here for the last ten years, this is my home now. But even I think about heading back to the USA from time to time. Life out here is hard.'

'So why do you stay?'

'To be honest, I have no idea. I guess I just can't think of a good enough reason to leave. It's not like I have family or the love of a good woman waiting for me to return to.'

'You're not married?' Kirstin asked.

Hanson chuckled. 'You think anybody would have me?'

'Have you ever been married?' she said.

'Once, a couple of years back,' Hanson replied. 'Didn't work out.'

Kirstin got the feeling he didn't want to talk about it, and so she kept quiet.

Hanson glanced over his shoulder at Naomi. 'You should be wearing your seatbelt.'

'Why? Is Janice going to crash or something?'

'Hey, Janice never — '

A sharp pang of fear shot through Kirstin's stomach as the plane's engine stuttered and coughed. 'What's happening?'

Hanson leaned forward and tapped

at the fuel gauge. The needle showed empty. 'I don't understand, she should have a full tank of fuel.'

The engine coughed again and then fell silent. Kirstin looked out of her window. The propeller had stopped spinning.

'I don't believe it,' Hanson said. 'A bullet must have hit the fuel tank. Hold on to your hats, ladies, we're going down!'

4

In the back seat, Naomi screamed. 'What's she screaming for?' Hanson yelled.

Kirstin looked anxiously down at the green canopy of trees below them swaying in the wind and lashed with rain. 'You just told her we're going to crash!'

'I did not say we're going to crash, I said we're going down!'

From what Kirstin could see, that sounded like it was the same thing. The rainforest below them was dense. How on earth was Hanson going to find them a clearing to land in? The tops of the trees sped by, and it seemed to Kirstin that already they were closer than they had been a moment ago. The plane was gliding, buffeted by the wind and steadily losing altitude.

And there was nothing they could do to stop it.

'Has your daughter got her seatbelt

on?' Hanson said.

Kirstin glanced back. Naomi had her seatbelt strapped tight across her midriff and was clutching her seat, her eyes screwed shut.

'Yes, she has.' Kirstin faced forward. 'Are we going to die?'

'Not today,' Hanson said, his face set with a grim determination. 'See the river up ahead? If I can land Janice in the water . . .'

Kirstin peered through the rainstreaked windscreen. She could just see the wide river, cutting through the forest. It seemed an awfully long way off. And still further away, beyond the river and the forest and shrouded in mist and cloud cover, were the mountains. Those mountains had been Kirstin's destination.

The rainforest seemed to fill the windscreen as they dropped lower and lower. Hanson pulled back at the controls, struggling to keep them airborne. But without power, he was fighting a losing battle.

The plane skimmed across the top of

the highest trees, the branches and leaves catching on the undercarriage.

'We're not going to make it!' Hanson shouted. 'Get ready, this isn't gonna be pretty!'

Kirstin couldn't remember much of what happened next.

She remembered hearing Naomi scream. Hanson throwing his hands up in the air as a branch twisted its way into the plane's cabin.

And she remembered everything going dark.

And she remembered thinking, I'm going to die.

★ ★ ★

Kirstin groaned. Why did she hurt so much?

And then it all came flooding back.

They were in the plane, which was jammed at an angle in the tops of the trees. Thick branches enclosed them, trapping them in place. The windscreen had shattered and Kirstin realised she was covered in glass fragments. The wind tugged at her clothes and rain drops hit her face.

'Naomi! Are you alright? Are you hurt?'

'No, I'm fine, I think,' Naomi replied.

Kirstin looked at Hanson. He lay slumped in his seat, his head lolling over his chest. His forehead had a red gash across it. Was he dead?

Kirstin reached out a trembling hand and touched his arm.

Hanson flinched and snapped open his eyes. 'What the . . . ? Where . . . ?' He looked at Kirstin and the confusion cleared from his eyes. 'Oh.'

A groan shivered through the plane as it shifted position. 'We need to get out of here,' Hanson said, groggily. He reached up and wrenched the door open. 'We're a long way up. How are you both at climbing?'

'I suppose we're going to find out,' Kirstin said. They all unclipped their seat belts. The plane made grating noises against the branches as it shifted with each movement they made.

'Is the plane going to fall out of the trees?' Naomi asked anxiously.

'I don't think so,' Hanson replied. 'These trees are strong and closely packed together. I doubt we're going anywhere.'

He lifted a leg out of the cockpit and placed it gingerly on the wing. The plane shifted again, the branches and leaves stirring. Something chattered and called out in the distance. Kirstin had no idea what it might be, but she didn't like the sound of it.

'We're wedged in tight,' Hanson said, hanging on the lip of the cockpit door and looking down. 'But the good news is, there is a thick branch here we can use to start climbing down.' He looked into the flight cabin. 'Naomi, let's get you out of there next.'

From the expression on her face, Naomi looked like she would prefer to just stay right where she was, but she reached out and grabbed Hanson's extended hand and allowed him to pull her out.

'Here, hang on to this.' Hanson guided her hand to a thick branch, dripping with moisture.

Naomi closed her hand around it and pulled a face in disgust. 'It's yucky.'

'I know, but you're just going to have to ignore it,' Hanson said. 'You need to use that branch to climb down until you get to the main trunk just down there. See it?' Hanson pointed through the swaying foliage.

Naomi nodded.

'Okay, you need to get moving, just take it slow and easy and you'll be fine.'

Naomi nodded again, but stayed right where she was.

'Naomi?' Kirstin said.

Naomi looked at her mother, eyes wide with fear. 'It's a long way down.'

'I know darling, but we need to get out of the plane and down on the ground.'

Naomi nodded and started moving.

Hanson watched her for a few moments and then turned to Kristin. 'Okay, your turn.' He reached out a hand.

49

Kirstin took it and he pulled her out of her seat. He was strong, and his grip was firm but not painful. Kirstin climbed on to the wing and checked on Naomi, who was having to push her way through a dense wall of leaves to get to the trunk.

'Are you alright?' Hanson said.

Kirstin nodded.

'Okay, follow Naomi, but be careful.'

'I will,' Kirstin said, and began inching her way along the branch towards Naomi.

The branch was sticky beneath her hands and water dripped on her from leaves over her head. The noise of the rain was a constant barrage around her. She had to push through the dense foliage to reach the tree's massive trunk, and each time she did the branches and leaves showered her with more water.

Kirstin's face dripped with sweat, mingling with the raindrops, and her top clung to her back.

She suddenly remembered the rucksacks. They couldn't leave those behind. But when she turned her head to talk to Hanson, she saw him pulling the two bags out of the plane and slinging one over each shoulder. As Hanson pulled himself onto the branch, the plane shifted again with a metallic groan. And she noticed a thin spiral of smoke drifting from the engine.

'Mr Hanson?' Kirstin pointed.

Hanson didn't even turn around to look. 'Yeah, I know. Just keep moving.'

In front of Kirstin, Naomi had reached the tree's massive trunk and was hugging it like she loved it desperately.

'Naomi, you're going to have to start climbing down,' Kirstin called out. 'You have to make way for me and Mr Hanson.'

Without turning to look at her mother, Naomi began feeling for footholds and handholds. Fortunately, there were many branches at hand. Kirstin briefly wondered what kind of tree this was but then dismissed the thought in favour of concentrating on staying alive.

Kirstin reached the trunk next. She could hardly believe how thick it was.

And sticky.

Where did all this goo come from? Was it the sap from the tree? Or something else? A shrill scream snapped Kirstin from her thoughts.

'Naomi! What's wrong?'

'Ants!' Naomi yelled. 'Hundreds of giant ants!' Kirstin looked down and saw them.

A black stream of ants crawling over Naomi's hands as they scurried up the tree trunk.

'Just hold on!' Hanson yelled. 'They'll leave you alone as long as you don't move.'

The giant ants were headed straight for Kirstin. She couldn't believe how brave Naomi was, clinging to the trunk and so very still, like a statue.

But Kirstin? Oh, how she hated creepy crawlies.

The first of the ants reached her hand. Her knuckles were white with the tension of gripping the sticky bark. The red ants, their bodies bulbous and glistening, began crawling over Kirstin's hand.

Their legs pricked at her flesh. Kirstin ground her teeth together and screwed her eyes shut.

Do not scream. Do not scream.

Because if she did scream, she knew that she would completely lose control. And she would slip and fall. She just had to stay still. That was all. Just stay still until they had all passed on their way elsewhere. Easy.

Until they changed direction and began crawling up her arm. She snapped her eyes open. It seemed to Kirstin that suddenly their heads became magnified in her vision, and all she could see were their eyes and their pincers.

Kirstin couldn't hold the scream inside any longer. Pulling her hand away from the tree trunk, she shook her arm in an attempt to dislodge the ants and opened her mouth and screamed. The ants on the trunk started going crazy, their neat formation broken as they scattered. Kirstin was still shaking her arm violently when she realised she was losing her grip on the tree's bark.

'Kirstin!'

Hanson's yell was the last thing she heard before she found herself hanging on to nothing. For a tiny moment in time she was floating in space, and then leaves and thin branches were scratching at her face and arms as she plummeted towards the ground.

She smacked into something solid.

The impact winded her, and before Kirstin had time to wonder at how close the ground had been, she was sliding through the dense foliage. All of a sudden she realised she wasn't on the ground. The wing of the plane had blocked her fall, but now she was sliding down it and she would fall again with nothing to stop her but the ground far below. Kirstin grabbed at the wing, at its smooth metal surface. The sticky goo covering her hands slowed her down, but she was still sliding. She tried to get purchase with her feet, but they kicked into thin air, hanging over the edge of the wing.

A hand grabbed her shirt. Kirstin slid a little more and then stopped as her shirt gathered up and held her beneath her arms.

Kirstin looked up.

'I've got you,' Naomi said, sitting with her legs wrapped around a branch and holding onto another over her head.

Kirstin made a grab for the tree and held it tight. Kirstin let go.

'Is everyone okay?' Hanson called from above.

'We're both fine,' Naomi shouted.

Kirstin looked up, but she could hardly see Hanson through all the greenery. But she did see a flash of orange and more smoke.

'The plane is on fire,' she said.

'I know,' Hanson replied. 'We need to get moving, and quickly!'

They didn't waste any time. Kirstin looked down. There were plenty of branches to use for footholds and hand-holds. She started climbing, with Naomi closely following.

'Look out below!' Hanson cried.

A moment later, with a crashing and snapping, Kirstin's heavy rucksack fell through the snarl of branches and creeping vines, just missing her as it plummeted towards the ground. Kirstin heard it hit the forest floor with a thud and a splash.

'Sorry!' Hanson called out.

They began climbing again, lowering themselves carefully, but as swiftly as they could, towards safety on the ground.

Finally, Kirstin had to stop.

She had run out of branches to step on. She could see the ground now, and her rucksack. But solid earth was at least twenty feet away.

A sudden crashing and splintering had Kirstin craning her head back and looking up.

'It's the plane!' Hanson yelled. 'The fire is burning away the branches holding it in place. Get out of the way before it falls on top of us!'

Suddenly she could see it, falling towards her in a jerking, halting motion as it snapped through the branches. It was so big it seemed to be swallowing up the sky as it grew bigger and bigger.

Kirstin looked down again. The

ground still seemed like an awfully long way off.

'You've got to jump, Mum!' Naomi said.

'No, we'll lower ourselves,' Kirstin replied.

She turned on her front and lowered herself off the branch. Her legs kicked and swung and Kirstin had to will them to stay still. Gripping the branch tight, she lowered herself until her arms were extended above her head. Another loud crash from above forced Kirstin to let go.

Again she fell. But the bone-crunching landing she expected didn't happen. Instead, the ground almost seemed to swallow her up, like a sponge.

'It's alright!' she shouted up to Naomi. 'The ground is soft and muddy!'

Naomi dropped from her perch in the tree and landed beside Kirstin. Before she had time to say anything, Hanson landed beside the two women in a tangle of limbs.

Above them the plane crashed its way through more branches, showering the three of them with leaves and splinters of smoking bark. Hanson climbed to his feet. 'Come on, let's get out of the way before that thing drops on our heads.'

Kirstin stood up too and looked at Naomi who was still sitting down.

'My leg's caught in something!' she gasped.

She was right. Kirstin could see her foot was being held down by creeping vines that seemed to have wrapped themselves around Naomi's ankle. Both Kirstin and Hanson grabbed at her leg and began pulling. The plane smashed its way further down in a halting, jerky motion. It ground to a halt as it snagged on something. Kirstin glanced up. She saw that one of the wings had been ripped off and was lodged precariously behind the plane. Sweat poured down Hanson's face and dripped from his chin as he yanked at the green vines and roots strangling Naomi's ankle.

Kirstin heard the plane shift again. Naomi screamed. With a final agonising tearing noise, the plane hurtled for them.

Kirstin threw herself over her daughter in a desperate attempt to shield her from harm as Hanson continued to fight with the tangle of creepers around Naomi's ankle.

The plane screeched to a halt once more, the sound enveloping them. Kirstin waited a second as scraps of debris fell on her.

She looked up. The plane was pointed down, its nose only a few feet away, hanging above them.

'There, I got it!' Hanson gasped as Naomi was suddenly able to wriggle her foot free.

The three of them scurried away as the plane dropped again and landed on its nose with a deafening crash in the spot they had just left. It settled its undercarriage against the side of the massive tree. Kirstin fell on her back in the mud and let out a ragged sigh of relief.

5

Hot, filthy and tired, they stumbled their way through the jungle until they found a spot where they could rest. Kirstin wiped her sleeve across her forehead. Strings of damp hair hung over her eyes and she pushed them back. She needed a shower, but she wasn't going to get one. At least the rain had stopped for the moment.

'We're going to die out here, aren't we?' Naomi said.

Kirstin took her hand and squeezed it. 'No, honey, we're not. We'll be okay, I promise.'

She looked at Hanson hopefully, needing a sign from him that she wasn't lying to her daughter.

'Your mother's right,' he said. 'You hear that noise?'

Kirstin cocked her head and listened. She realised she could hear rushing water, somewhere off to her left. 'Is that the river we saw?'

Hanson nodded. 'And I saw a jetty on its south bank, not too far from here, and a couple of outbuildings. We should be able to find help there.'

'Is it really going to be that easy?'

'Well, maybe not easy, we could have a long walk ahead of us. But yeah, it's that simple.'

Naomi stood up. 'Shall we go then?'

Hanson stood up and hoisted the backpack over his shoulder. 'I don't see why not.'

Kirstin climbed wearily to her feet too.

Hanson led the way, forcing a route through the dense forest. It seemed like nature had turned against them for invading its space. Creeping vines and roots snagged at their feet and their ankles, hanging vines pulled at their clothes and hair, and all around them was the sound of screeching birds. But all the time they heard the river, the sound of rushing water growing louder as they drew closer to it.

Finally they reached the riverbank.

The water flowed fast, and the river was wide. Hanson decided that they should head upriver.

They trudged along the river bank in a single file, Hanson at the front and Kirstin at the back.

After a couple of hours of tedious walking, Hanson spotted a building ahead through the trees. They picked up their pace.

'That's it, that's the place I saw.'

There was a rickety, wooden pier stretching out over the water. Old tyres had been tied to the thick, wooden poles to act as a buffer for boats docking at the pier. A battered old boat complete with a cabin and a deck was tied to the jetty. On the riverbank sat a wooden shack with one door and a window. The space out front was littered with engine parts and empty sacks, lengths of timber and old, discoloured barrels.

Hanson rapped his knuckles on the door.

A grizzled old man with a pipe clenched between his teeth opened the door. His overalls were covered with oil and dirt. He looked at the three of them and then he craned his head and looked over their shoulders at the jetty.

'Where's your vessel?' he said. At least, that's what Kirstin thought he said. His Scottish accent was so thick it was almost impenetrable.

'We didn't come on the river,' Hanson said. 'We were flying, we had engine failure and crashed.'

'Ah, that was you making all that noise, was it?' The old man squinted at them from behind the cloud of blue smoke drifting from his pipe. He stuck out his hand. 'The name's Moses McMickle, but you can call me Mo.'

Hanson made the rest of the introductions.

'We need transport, the nearest town will do, anywhere we can hitch a lift back to civilisation,' he said.

'You've come to the right place,' Moses said, hitching his trousers up. 'I'm expecting a boat later this afternoon. You might be able to grab a ride with them.'

'Do you know where they're headed?'

'Aye, deep into the heart of the jungle,' Moses replied.

'That's the wrong way for us,' Hanson said.

'No, it isn't,' Kirstin said. She grabbed her rucksack and unzipped it. After rooting around inside it, she pulled out a folded sheet of paper. She laid it out on a table. 'Is this the river we're on?' She pointed at a line snaking through the hand-drawn map.

'Aye.' Moses nodded.

Kirstin turned to Hanson. 'Then that's where we need to get to.'

'Uh-uh.' Hanson shook his head. 'What's all this we business? I need to get back, buy myself a new plane to replace poor Janice.'

'You're going to leave me here?'

'Hey, that's your decision. You can come back with me if you want to.'

'I'll come back with you,' Naomi said.

'Oh no, you're staying with me, young woman!'

'Mum!' Naomi put her hands on her

64

hips and stared at her mother.

'Don't look at me like that,' Kirstin said.

'But I want to go home, back to England and back to school.'

'Well you should have thought of that earlier, shouldn't you? Like maybe before you started beating that poor boy up!'

'I told you, I didn't beat him up, we were fighting.'

'What were you fighting over?' Hanson said.

'It doesn't matter,' Naomi said, turning her back on Hanson and staring at her mother. 'I want you to take me home right now.'

'No,' Kirstin said.

'This is ridiculous. You're supposed to be the adult around here, but you're acting like a spoilt teenager.'

Kirstin turned away and looked out at the river. Maybe Naomi was right. Kirstin had put her daughter in direct danger by bringing her here, but what else was she supposed to do?

Not come at all.

But that hadn't been an option. With the knowledge she had gained from her grandfather's journal, Kirstin now had the best opportunity of her life to find the Lost City of Quetzalcoatl.

And Kirstin didn't just want to find it.

She needed to. 'You said there are some people coming through later?' Kirstin said to Moses.

Moses rubbed his chin, the stubble making a sandpaper sound against his hand. 'Aye, that's right, young lady. How far do you plan on going?'

'All the way.'

Hanson rounded on Kirstin. 'Are you serious? Have you got a death wish or something?'

Kirstin ignored him. 'Naomi, you can go back with Mr Hanson. He will get you to a hotel and you can call granddad from there. You're right, I should never have brought you along with me, but you're going home now.'

Naomi looked down at the ground. 'I don't want to go home, not without you. Why can't you come back with me?'

'You know the kid's right — '

'Was I talking to you?' Kirstin snapped.

Hanson turned his back on Kirstin and stalked to the end of the jetty.

Kirstin's heart sank as she watched Hanson standing with his back to her. Why was she shouting at this man who had just saved their lives? Not once, but twice. She should have been thanking him, not yelling in his face. What was wrong with her? Had Charles' betrayal warped her in some way, had it turned her bitter and angry?

Kirstin was pulled from her thoughts by the touch of Naomi's hand in hers. 'Mum? Please, can't we go home?'

Kirstin tried to smile, but her lips trembled and she could feel hot tears gathering in her eyelids. Maybe she was right, maybe Charles' betrayal had changed her for the worse. This ridiculous trip into the heart of the jungle, and danger, had become less about finding Quetzalcoatl, and more about beating Charles and Julia to it.

Wasn't that the reason? Had Kirstin

become so bitter because of Charles's betrayal that she was willing not only to risk her own life, but her daughter's in an attempt to get revenge? Already today they had been shot at by men chasing them and then almost died in a plane crash. Taking a deep breath, Kirstin closed her eyes. Maybe it was time to take a step back and reassess what was important in her life.

Kirstin opened her eyes and squeezed Naomi's hand. 'Hey, when did you get so grown up and sensible, huh? You're right, we should go home.'

Naomi grinned and then threw her arms around her mum and gave her a big hug.

'Mr Hanson!' Kirstin called out. 'You've got what you wanted, we're going home.'

Hanson, standing on the jetty, turned to face them. 'Alright, now you're talking sense.'

★ ★ ★

Moses agreed to take them downriver to the nearest village where they could hire transport back to civilisation. He wasn't too happy about it as he was meant to be restocking and refuelling the boat he was waiting for, but he decided to stack everything they needed on the jetty and take payment when he met them going upriver.

Hanson helped him with the supplies and then they all climbed into his boat, a ramshackle old tub which belched black smoke from its chimney when he started the engine up.

'Is this thing seaworthy?' Hanson shouted over the throb of the engine and pulling Kirstin from her thoughts.

'Aye, it is that,' Moses said. 'And I'd thank you not to insult my Bessie.'

'Bessie?' Naomi said, rolling her eyes. 'Does everyone out here have to give their planes and boats names?'

Kirstin burst out laughing. And that felt good. Seemed like she hadn't laughed for a long time.

'Hold on,' Hanson said as Bessie

began floating away from the jetty. 'I'm not convinced Bessie is as reliable as Moses believes.'

The engine backfired and belched an even dirtier cloud of smoke into the air.

Hanson sat down beside Kirstin. 'You know this river is infested with crocodiles, don't you?'

Kirstin gave him a disapproving stare. 'Are you trying to scare me, Mr Hanson?'

'What's with all this Mr Hanson business? You almost make me sound like a respectable business man.'

Kirstin burst out laughing. 'I'm not sure that's even possible.'

'Yeah, well, you can call me Josh, that's what everyone else does.' He held out his hand.

Kirstin took it and they shook. 'Pleased to meet you, Josh. I'm Kirstin, and that's Naomi.'

Josh looked over at Naomi standing by the boat's prow, looking out at the river. 'She's a brave kid, coming out here with you.'

'She is,' Kirstin said. 'In fact, she's stronger than most people realise. She's been through a lot in her life so far.'

'That whole wedding day thing must have been tough for her, as well as you.'

Kirstin nodded slowly. 'But she already knew, she'd told me so often that Charles wasn't right for me, and I just thought it was jealousy, that she was scared of losing me.'

'But it turned out she'd seen right through him after all.' Josh chuckled. 'I could have done with her advice too.'

There it was again, that sense of hurt in his past. Of something that he was running from.

'What do you mean?' Kirstin asked, gently probing. She didn't want to intrude, but it seemed to Kirstin as though he was ready to open up and talk about the obvious hurt in his life.

Josh took a deep breath and let it out in a sigh. 'Oh, nothing really. We've all got history, right?'

Kirstin nudged him gently with her elbow. 'Come on Mr Hanson, you're

71

holding back on me. I've told you my story.'

'There's not a lot to tell,' Josh said, his head bowed as he gazed at the boat's aged deck. 'I met a woman, I fell hard for her, we got married.' Josh fell silent and Kirstin waited for him to continue.

'I came home early from work one day, and there she was,' he said finally. 'There she was.'

Kirstin didn't need to ask for any more details. She'd been there, she knew what he'd interrupted. 'It hurts, doesn't it?' she said. 'That kind of betrayal, it hurts more than anything else in the world.'

'It sure does,' Josh replied. 'We'd hardly been married any time at all, we'd hardly been together any time at all. It was like she exploded into my life and then she was gone again in no time, leaving me to pick up the pieces.'

'And then you came out here?'

Josh nodded. 'That's right. Seemed like I didn't have time for other people anymore.'

'But other people didn't hurt you, just

the one,' Kirstin said. 'Are you going to let your ex-wife's betrayal of you shape the rest of your life?'

Hanson raised an eyebrow. 'I thought you were an archaeologist, not a counsellor.'

Kirstin smiled. 'I just don't like seeing someone unhappy. It makes me sad too.'

'There's a boat heading towards us!' Naomi called out.

'That'll be the crew I was telling you about, needing to resupply,' Moses shouted over the throb of the engine. 'Let me pull in and I can explain the situation to them.'

Naomi hurried over to her mother and sat down beside her.

'What's wrong?' Kirstin said.

'There's a man standing at the front of the boat,' Naomi replied. 'He's big, and . . . I don't like the look of him.'

With a thud, the other boat knocked into them.

'Just tie her up there for a moment!' Moses called.

The engine fell silent and Moses

stepped out of his cabin.

The tallest man Kirstin had ever seen stepped onto Moses' boat. His skin was tanned and leathery, and he had a long jaw and deep-set eyes. And there was something else, something mean-spirited about his appearance. Kirstin could see why Naomi hadn't liked the look of him.

'I don't believe it!' Josh exclaimed, as two more people stepped on to the boat. 'Julia? What are you doing here?'

Kirstin's heart felt like it might stutter to a stop. It couldn't be. There were lots of people called Julia in the world, millions. It couldn't be . . .

Kirstin stood up.

'Charles?' she said.

'Well, what a coincidence,' Charles Dewberry said, and grinned.

'It certainly is,' Julia purred as she gazed at Josh.

6

Kirstin's legs seemed to have turned into wobbly tubes of rubber. All she wanted right now was to sit down before she fell down, but she couldn't. Not with Charles and Julia watching. Kirstin's pride wouldn't let her.

'This is your ex-wife?' she said, pointing at her cousin.

'I'm afraid so,' Josh replied, and it sounded like he was spitting the words out.

Charles Dewberry tipped his head back and laughed. 'What an amazing coincidence!' He turned to Julia. 'So this is the man you have been telling me about? Julia, how could you?'

Julia arched a perfectly formed eyebrow. 'He had certain qualities I enjoyed.'

Dewberry chuckled and shook his head with amusement. 'Well, Kirstin, I have to say that it is nice to see you again, even taking into account the circumstances.'

'I can't say the same about you,' Kirstin said. 'Either of you.'

'Ah, Kirstin, I'm sorry you had to find Julia and myself in such an embarrassing situation on our wedding day, but let's face it, our marriage never would have worked, would it?' Dewberry said. 'The two of us, we're just too similar, too competitive.'

'I'm nothing like you,' Kirstin snarled. 'And I'm glad I found out who you really are, I just wish it had been sooner. Naomi had the measure of you, I should have listened to her.'

Dewberry looked over Kirstin's shoulder at Naomi, still huddled by the side of the boat. 'Naomi, how lovely to see you here. Aren't you going to come and say hello?'

Naomi turned her head away.

'What are you doing here, Charles?' Kirstin said.

'What do you think?' Charles said. 'I'm looking for the Lost City of Quetzalcoatl, just like you.'

'But that's not possible, that's not . . .'

Kirstin's voice trailed off. 'Did you send those men with guns after us?'

'Well, I wouldn't say I sent them after you, exactly,' Dewberry said.

'What does that mean?' Kirstin said.

'It means he got drunk in a seedy bar one night and blabbed his mouth off,' Julia interrupted. 'Once those men found out about the legend of the treasures in the Lost City, they got it into their heads to find you and make you tell them where it is.'

'It really was rather unfortunate,' Dewberry said, and laughed. 'But I'm glad we ran into each other, you can save me a lot of bother.'

Kirstin backed up a step. She didn't like the sound of this. 'What do you mean?'

'You know exactly what I mean, Kirstin.' Dewberry held out his hand. 'Give me the map.'

Kirstin didn't move. 'How did you find out about the map?'

Dewberry shrugged. 'I have my ways.'

'And how did you find out where we

77

are?'

'The map, Kirstin,' Dewberry said, his voice growing soft and menacing. 'Give me the map.'

'No.'

Dewberry lifted a hand and crooked his finger at the tall man who had boarded the boat first. 'Oddball, search their rucksacks.'

Kirstin's rucksack looked like a toy in Oddball's massive hands. He yanked the rucksack open and tipped it upside down. The contents dropped to the deck. Kirstin took a step towards Oddball, but Josh grabbed her arm and held her back.

Oddball rotated his head and glowered at them with his deep-set eyes. 'Where'd you find your pet Rottweiler?' Josh said. 'The circus?'

'Now, don't be unkind, Mr Hanson,' Dewberry said. 'I think you will find that Oddball has a very gentle nature.'

Oddball began rooting through the pile of Kirstin's belongings. Naomi had gathered her rucksack to her and hugged it to her chest.

'How are you, Joshua?' Julia said. 'Still flying tourists over the rainforest in that rusty tin can you call a plane?'

'Janice might have been a rusty old tin can, but she was a lot more reliable than you,' Josh replied.

'Might have been?' Julia said. 'You mean you don't own it anymore?'

'There was . . . an incident.'

Oddball stood up, a journal clutched in his huge hand.

'No!' Kirstin shouted, and Josh had to hold her back. 'That was my grandfather's journal! You can't take that!'

Oddball handed the journal to Dewberry, who flipped through its pages.

'This is exactly what we want,' he said, turning to Julia.

Kirstin struggled to pull herself free from Josh's grip, but he was too strong.

'Julia!' she shouted. 'He was your grandfather too, you can't let Charles have it!'

'And why not?' Julia replied, smirking. She took the journal from Charles and leafed through it. 'This looks fascinating.'

Kirstin struggled against Josh's hold on her. 'Let go of me!'

'I can't do that,' Josh grunted.

Charles turned and spoke to Moses. Moses nodded and walked down to the end of the boat.

'Wait a minute, are you with these idiots too?' Josh said.

Moses didn't say anything, didn't even look at Josh. He got on his hands and knees and lifted a hatch in the deck.

'Once we realised where you were headed, I contacted Moses and asked him to delay you until we arrived,' Charles said. 'He was a little reluctant at first, but then I offered him a substantial amount of money and he soon changed his mind.'

Kirstin had stopped fighting to free herself from Josh's hold and he let go of her. 'How did you know where we were headed?' she said.

Charles ignored Kirstin and turned to Julia. 'We should go now. These two have outlived their usefulness.'

Julia smiled. 'Joshua did that a long

time ago.'

The two of them climbed back on to their boat. Oddball stayed where he was, keeping an eye on Kirstin and Josh. It seemed he was waiting until Moses had finished whatever he was doing.

Back on his boat, Charles turned and said, 'Oddball, grab their backpacks, will you?'

'No!' Kirstin shouted. 'You can't!'

Oddball yanked Naomi's backpack from her grip and threw it through the air in a graceful arc onto Charles' boat. Then he scooped up Kirstin's belongings off the deck where he had dumped them, shoving them back into the rucksack. He threw that to Charles as well.

Kirstin watched in silence. She knew there was no point in protesting, or appealing to Charles' better nature. He didn't have one.

'Moses, what's going on?' Josh said. 'What are you doing?'

Moses dropped the deck hatch closed and stood up. 'I'm sorry, Mr Hanson.'

'Moses!' Josh yelled. 'What have you

done?'

Moses couldn't meet Josh's gaze. He untethered the boat and then jumped onto Dewberry's vessel. Oddball joined them.

A gap opened up between the two boats and began to widen.

'Goodbye, Kirstin!' Dewberry yelled, raising a hand in farewell. 'I hope never to see you again.'

Moses' boat, Bessie, began to twist in the river's current as it took them downstream.

'Keep to the left bank and you'll be fine!' Moses shouted.

'What's he talking about?' Kirstin asked, as the boat picked up speed.

'I don't know,' Josh muttered. 'But I sure don't like the sound of it.'

Josh scrambled over to the engine hatch and pulled it open. He lay down on his front and peered into the space. 'Oh no.' He looked up Kirstin. 'Moses has removed the drive belt from the engine. We can't go anywhere now, except where the river wants to take us.'

Kirstin looked anxiously back at the other boat, swiftly receding into the distance. Only Moses stood at the stern, watching them. She turned back to Josh.

'Can you repair it?'

Josh shook his head. 'You don't understand, Moses has taken the drive belt. Unless he has a spare one on the boat which I seriously doubt, there's nothing we can do.'

'But where will we stop, where can we get off the boat and back on land?'

'Mum?' Naomi said. She had joined Kirstin and Josh and slipped her arm around Kirstin's waist.

Kirstin pulled her daughter closer.

'We can't,' Josh said. 'The river is just going to take us wherever it wants.' He paused and snapped his fingers. 'Wait, Moses said we should keep to the left bank. But why?'

He looked forward. The river was carrying them faster than ever.

'We're heading straight for the Aztenga Falls,' Josh said.

'Is that good?' Kirstin said, despite the

dreadful feeling she had in her stomach that no, it wasn't good at all.

'No, that's not good. In fact, it's terrible. But Moses said to keep to the left bank, because . . . ' he snapped his fingers again. 'Because there's a tributary just before the waterfall that will lead us to safety. But we have to keep to the left!'

Josh dashed for the wheelhouse and made a grab for the wheel. It was spinning out of control and he snatched his hand back with a yelp.

'That almost broke my fingers!'

The boat turned and twisted in the current.

'I feel sick,' Naomi said, and sat down on the deck.

Kirstin knew how she felt. They were twisting and swaying and hurtling downriver too fast.

Josh tried grabbing the spinning wheel again. This time he managed to hold on to it and wrestle it under his control.

'What happens if we miss the tributary?' Kirstin yelled.

'We'll head straight for the Aztenga

Falls with nothing to stop us!' Josh yelled, fighting to stop the boat's manic spinning.

'And then?'

'And then we just go right over the edge and plummet down a 150 foot drop and onto the rocks!'

Kirstin closed her eyes.

That wasn't the news she had wanted to hear.

7

Without a working engine they were completely in the water's power. Kirstin watched, helplessly, as the riverbanks flew by in a blur of motion. Sometimes the boat spun around and tipped and swayed, giving Kirstin a feeling of drunkenness.

But mostly they just hurtled downriver.

Josh wrestled with the wheel, fighting to keep the boat under his control.

'There's the channel,' Kirstin yelled. 'We're going to shoot past it!'

'I'm doing my best,' Josh grunted, hauling the boat's wheel round, vainly fighting the river's strength.

Kirstin gripped the boat's sides as they drew closer to the break in the river. If they could only steer into the channel where the water was calmer they would have a chance to steer into the bank and get onto the safety of land. That and they would avoid hurtling over the edge of a massive waterfall and smashing against the rocks at the bottom.

The boat began to turn into the bank as Josh managed to get some control.

'We're going to do it!' Kirstin yelled.

The break in the river drew closer. But Kirstin realised she had been wrong, and they were still too far away.

'We need to be closer!' Kirstin shouted, willing the boat closer to the bank speeding by.

'I'm trying,' Josh grunted.

Kirstin reached out an arm as they drew closer. Surely Josh could steer them into the channel and away from the waterfall?

The tributary approached and Kirstin let out a whoop of joy as she realised the boat's prow was now pointing in exactly the right direction.

'You did it!' she yelled. 'You did — '

With a deep thud from the hull, the boat juddered and spun off course.

'Oh no, we hit a rock!' Josh shouted.

He fought with the wheel again, but

then it snapped out of his grasp and began spinning out of control once more.

The three of them watched as they rushed past the river channel leading to calmer water and safety. They were helpless as their last chance at getting back on land disappeared. Kirstin looked ahead. Was that the sound of the waterfall she could hear already?

'How long before we get to the Aztenga Falls?' Kirstin said.

Josh, his face set in a grim scowl, replied, 'At this speed? I don't know, maybe another five minutes?'

Naomi was sitting on the deck, her head in her hands. The boat had begun to spin and sway once more.

'And there's nothing we can do?' Kirstin said.

Josh shook his head. 'Without that drive belt? Not a thing.'

'What about jumping over the side? Do you think we could swim to the riverbank?'

Josh shook his head again. 'Not a chance. This river is far too powerful.'

Kirstin tipped her head back and screamed. 'There has to be something we can do!' She pointed at the coils of rope lying on the deck. 'What if we made a lasso out of the rope and lassoed a branch or something?'

Josh thought for a second. 'We'd just get yanked out of the boat and right into the water.'

'But we could use it to pull ourselves to the riverbank.'

'It's crazy, we'd die.'

Kirstin punched him in the chest. 'Hey! I've got you news for you, mister! We're going to die, anyway!'

Josh picked up the coil of rope and began feeding it thoughtfully through his hands. 'It's the worst idea ever. I know what you're saying, but — ' Josh turned and looked at the engine.

'What?' Kirstin said, a glimmer of hope flowering in her chest. 'You've had an idea, what is it?'

'It's almost as stupid as your idea,' Josh muttered. 'But it might work, it just might.'

He spun around and grabbed Kirstin by her shoulder. The intensity of his gaze almost frightened her. 'Go find me a knife, quick.'

'A knife?'

But Josh didn't answer. He had already dropped to his knees on the deck and was peering into the engine space. A knife. There had to be one somewhere on this boat. Moses McMickle looked like the kind of man who would keep a knife somewhere, probably one of those big ones with a serrated edge and a carved, ivory handle. Something utilitarian but flashy too.

Kirstin ran inside the cabin. Pulled open cupboard doors. Tin plates, boxes of nuts and bolts, engine parts, and fishing wire fell onto the floor. The boat rocked from side to side. Kirstin looked up. Through the cabin window she saw the riverbank swinging past as the boat spun around in a sickening motion.

Concentrate! You can feel sick later when you're back on land.

Kirstin sorted through the detritus on

the cabin floor. There was no knife. She hauled herself to her feet and searched the cabin, her eyes probing every nook and cranny. There! Attached to the wooden wall, beneath a window. Why hadn't she seen it before? It was bigger than a knife, more like a hatchet, but surely it would do?

She snatched it from its place and stumbled back out to the deck as the boat tipped from side to side even more violently.

'Here!' she shouted.

Josh, still on his knees, turned and grabbed the hatchet. He plunged his head and shoulders through the open hatch, arms extended as he worked on the engine.

Kirstin grabbed onto the boat's side as they pitched forward violently and then righted again. Why were they rocking and swaying so much?

Kirstin looked down the fast-flowing river and found her answer.

'Josh?' she said. 'I can see the edge of the waterfall.'

'I know!' Josh shouted, still working furiously.

Kirstin couldn't take her eyes off the water flowing over the edge in a plume of spray. Beyond that edge, there was nothing but sky.

Naomi was still curled up in a corner of the boat, her arms over her head and her knees drawn up to her chin. Kirstin was about to sit down beside her and hug her when Josh pulled his head out of the engine hatch and shouted, 'Start the engine!'

Kirstin turned and scrambled back inside the cabin. She grabbed at the wheel, not even stopping to think about the harm it might do to her fingers. Thankfully she was able to hang on to it, but she had to use all her strength to keep it from whipping from her grip. Unable to help herself, she glanced back. The waterfall was terrifyingly close.

She reached for the key to turn the ignition.

Her hand closed around empty space. 'There's no ignition key!' she screamed.

Josh stumbled into the cabin. He pushed past Kirstin and ripped the panelling off beneath the wheel. A jumble of wires spilled out.

'Hold on to the wheel!' he yelled.

He ripped two of the wires out of their housings, exposing the copper threads. He twisted the two ends together and the starter motor whined into stuttering life. The engine caught and roared. Josh grabbed hold of a lever and pushed, opening up the throttle and sending the boat's engine racing. Purple smoke billowed from the chimney and engulfed the cabin windows.

Kirstin glanced back again. She could no longer see the waterfall, just the blue sky. They had to be right on the edge.

'Come on!' Josh shouted, leaning into the throttle. The boat was no longer being pulled to the edge of the waterfall. The propeller was fighting the current, and they began edging back up the river. Away from the edge of the waterfall, and the long drop to the rocks down below.

They sailed the boat upriver and docked at Moses' jetty. No-one spoke. It seemed to Kirstin like there was too much to say, that the enormity of what had just happened was too big to put into words. Twice now in less than twenty-four hours they had brushed close to death and escaped.

Josh had saved them both times.

Once they were far enough from the waterfall, and once the adrenaline had worn off, Kirstin had suffered a bout of shakes. Josh had made her sit down while he took control of the wheel. Now, back on land and safe, she felt much better.

Josh worked on attempting a proper repair of the boat's engine while Kirstin and Naomi took a walk on dry land. 'That was frightening, wasn't it?' she said to Naomi.

The teenage girl nodded. 'I thought we were going to die.'

'So did I.' Kirstin glanced back at Josh in the boat. 'But Josh saved us, didn't he?'

Naomi looked over her shoulder. 'He's amazing. You should marry him.'

Kirstin burst out laughing and Naomi joined in.

'We would drive each other crazy! You aren't serious, are you?'

Naomi shrugged. 'Maybe, maybe not.'

'Besides, you know I've sworn off men for the rest of my life. They're not worth it.'

'You don't mean that.'

'I do. They're liars and cheats, the lot of them.'

'Do you really mean that?' Naomi said.

Kirstin paused and looked at her daughter. Naomi had her whole life ahead of her. It wasn't fair of Kirstin to be souring her daughter's view of relationships so early in her life. She had to make her own mistakes, find out the truth for herself. And who knew? Maybe Naomi would find herself a man who was the exception to the rule. One who would love her and respect her, treat her well.

'No, I don't mean it,' Kirstin said, hoping that Naomi wouldn't see the lie. 'I'm just being cynical because I feel hurt still. I don't love Charles one bit, and I can see now that I never actually did. I suppose I was on the rebound from your dad upping and leaving like he did when you were a baby. But still, even though I have nothing but contempt for Charles, it still hurts to see him with that cousin of mine.'

Kirstin paused, thinking about how one husband had left her and another had betrayed her. Maybe she should be careful about souring Naomi's view of men and relationships, but Kirstin doubted she could ever trust a man again.

Except, Josh, he seemed different didn't he? He was strong, reliable, resourceful. Kirstin couldn't imagine he would ever betray someone.

Kirstin scolded herself, suddenly angry that she was thinking this way about another man. Especially one she had only met a few hours ago,

'And do you think he meant us to go over that waterfall when he set us loose in the river?' Naomi said, breaking Kirstin's train of thought.

'What?' Kirstin said.

'Charles, do you think he meant to send us over the waterfall?'

'I don't think so,' Kirstin replied. 'I couldn't see even Charles stooping that low and doing something like that.'

'But it was Moses who told us to keep left on the river, not Charles.'

'I know, but still . . .' Was it possible? Were Charles and Julia prepared to kill, in order to get to the Lost City first?

They started walking again. Kirstin took hold of Naomi's hand.

'I'm sorry I brought you here with me,' she said. 'The last thing I wanted was for you to be in danger.'

'That's okay. It's been fun.'

'Fun? Really?'

'Well, sort of.'

'Anyway, I've decided,' Kirstin said. 'We're going home, back to the UK.'

Naomi pulled her hand away. 'Mum!'

'What?'

Naomi held out her hands by her sides. 'We can't go home, not now that Charles and Julia are here. We can't let them find the Lost City first.'

'Well, this is a turn up for the books,' Kirstin said. 'I thought you wanted to go back?'

'I did, but not anymore. We need to find the Lost City of Quetzalcoatl. That's what you came here to do, right?'

'Well, yes, but . . . '

Naomi placed her hands on her hips. 'But nothing. We're doing this for Grand-dad. He wouldn't have wanted a pair of idiots like Charles and Julia to be the ones to find the city. It belongs to us.'

'Naomi, the Lost City belongs to no-one.'

'Mum, you know what I mean. If Charles and Julia find it first, they will just loot it of all the treasures, you know they will.'

Kirstin mulled this over for a few moments. She had been taken aback by Naomi's response. It surprised her and pleased her. But still . . .

'No, I can't put you in any more danger than I already have,' she said. 'We're going home.'

'But what about Charles and Julia?' Naomi wailed. 'We can't let them take all the glory for finding the Lost City. They never would have got this far if it wasn't for us!'

'I know, I know, but we'll just have to live with it. Besides, I've been thinking for a while now of moving jobs, and going somewhere I know I won't ever have to see Charles' smug face ever again.'

'That's just so not fair!' Naomi said. 'When I didn't want to come on this stupid trip you made me, and now I want to stay you're telling me I've got to go home. I wish you would just make up your mind!'

Naomi spun on her heels and walked away. Kirstin watched her, thinking of how grown up she was becoming, but how much of a child she still was. Naomi was right, Kirstin never should have brought her daughter here, to the rainforest. It had been stupid and reckless.

But now they were here, how on earth was Kirstin going to persuade Naomi to leave?

In the end, the decision was made for them.

'We can't use Moses' boat anymore,' Josh said, and pointed.

Bessie was sitting lopsided in the river, like a drunk at the end of a long party.

'Is it sinking?' Kirstin asked.

Josh nodded grimly. 'That rock we hit must have damaged the hull. There's no way that thing is getting us anywhere.'

'So what are we going to do?' Naomi said.

'Go back upriver.' Josh said. 'Follow your friends.'

Kirstin shook her head. 'Absolutely not.'

'We don't have a choice, Kirstin.'

'You saw what they did to us! They tried to kill us!' Kirstin yelled. 'And now you want to give them another chance?'

'If we stay here, we will die.'

'And if we follow them, we may well die!'

'Kirstin, they're kitted out for an expedition into the heart of the Amazon rainforest, and we're not. We're not even kitted out for a hike in a park. If we want to get access to food and water and shelter, and believe me we're going to need all of those things sooner rather than later, then we need to catch up with your ex.'

'And then what?' Kirstin said, throwing her arms in the air. 'We just walk right up to them and say, 'Hey, can we have some of your food and water, and maybe share a tent with you?''

Josh shrugged sheepishly. 'If anyone's got a better idea, I'm willing to listen.'

Kirstin sighed. She didn't have a better idea.

'If we set off now, we might be able to catch up with them before nightfall,' Josh said.

Kirstin placed her hands on her hips. 'But how do you know that? They've got a boat and we're on foot.'

'Not too far upriver is another set of falls. They'll be on foot by now too.'

'But they've had a good head start on us.'

'I know, but they've got a lot of kit to carry, which will have slowed them down. But us three — '

'Yeah, I know, we've got no kit at all, so at least we can move faster,' Kirstin said. 'Alright, you win.'

Josh gave Kirstin a crooked grin, and for a brief, fleeting moment she forgot all about their problems.

'Don't worry,' he said. 'I'm going to get you two back to civilisation safe and sound.'

8

The three of them walked along the riverbank in silence. The day had grown hot and flies buzzed constantly around Kirstin's face. Kirstin swiped and batted at them, but still they landed on her cheeks and forehead. They soon reached the waterfall that Josh had talked about. Gathering by the wall of water, they paused to appreciate the cool, fine spray on their faces and arms.

'Now we need to climb,' Josh said, pointing at the route beside the waterfall.

It wasn't exactly a path. More like an irregular clearing through the tangle of trees and vines. Some of it looked as though it had been cleared only hours ago.

At least Charles and Julia are having to do the hard work of hacking a route for the rest of us, Kirstin thought.

With all their equipment, plus the

rucksacks that they had stolen from Kirstin and Naomi, Charles and his gang had a lot to manhandle up the side of the waterfall. Josh was right, they would be making only very slow progress.

Josh led the way with Kirstin and Naomi trailing behind. Eventually they reached the top. Kirstin and Naomi collapsed on their backs on the flat rocks beside the river. Josh squatted on his haunches on the riverbank, watching the water flowing by.

'What are you looking at?' Kirstin said, throwing an arm over her eyes to block out the bright sunlight.

'The water,' he replied. 'I just wish we had some to drink.'

Kirstin closed her eyes. She couldn't bear to think about drinking water or eating food right now. They needed to get up and get moving again. Once they caught up with Charles, they could have food and drink. If they could work out how to get it off him and his freakishly large bodyguard, Oddball.

'Let's get moving,' Josh said. 'We

haven't got long before nightfall.'

Kirstin and Naomi climbed wearily to their feet. Kirstin's feet were aching, and she was pretty sure she was developing blisters on her heels.

Josh looked as exhausted as Kirstin felt, but it was Naomi who was beginning to worry her. Naomi looked as though she was about to collapse from the effort of walking and climbing. And all without anything to drink or eat in the last couple of hours. Kirstin knew they had to find Charles soon, or they would be in trouble.

★ ★ ★

They found him only an hour later at a village by the side of the river. Darkness had fallen, but the village was alight with lanterns and fires. Josh and Kirstin watched from the shadows as Dewberry argued with a local man. A small crowd of children had formed around them and gazed up at the white man in fascination.

'What are they arguing about, do you think?' Kirstin whispered.

'Looks to me like your ex wants to hire a boat and they are haggling,' Josh replied.

'Typical,' Kirstin muttered. 'Charles is the richest person I have ever met, but he always has to haggle.'

'Mum, I'm really thirsty,' Naomi whispered.

'I know, darling, so am I,' Kirstin replied. 'We'll get something to drink very soon.'

'Looks like they have come to an agreement,' Josh said.

Kirstin saw Oddball and Julia loading bags onto the boat. 'There's my ruck-sack!'

'And mine!' Naomi hissed.

Kirstin turned to Josh. 'Alright, what's the plan?'

'Plan? Who said I had a plan?'

Kirstin jabbed Josh in the chest. 'Uh, you did!'

'I never said I had a plan,' Josh replied, looking down at the finger poking him in his chest. 'I might have said we needed a plan, but I most definitely did not say I had a plan. What about you?'

'Me? I don't have a plan!'

'Why not?'

'Are you serious?' Kirstin hissed. 'You're the man with the plans. You saved us from that crash, you saved us from falling over that waterfall, and you got us here. You're full of plans.'

'Hmm.' Josh rubbed his chin. 'I'd say that was more dumb luck than anything else. It certainly had nothing to do with plans.'

'You're so infuriating! You're supposed to know what you're doing.'

'Me? I don't know what I'm doing! I'm making it up as I go along.'

'Children, could you please stop arguing?' Naomi said. 'They're about to set off.'

Naomi was right. Charles was climbing on board the boat. It looked as though they weren't going to be resting anytime soon, but instead forging ahead. Kirstin had to do something. She couldn't let

Charles get away.

'Look, there's another boat tied up to the jetty,' Josh said. 'We're going to have to let them go, but then if we can hire that boat we can follow them.'

Kirstin didn't think that was the best plan she had ever heard, but Charles and Julia were already manoeuvring the boat into the middle of the river. She noticed Moses was still with them.

'Come on, let's get going,' Josh said.

They stood up and walked into the village. The buildings were all wooden and raised from the ground on poles and had thatched roofs. The children saw the newcomers and immediately dashed over to have a closer look. Some youngsters wore traditional tribal grass skirts, but others wore western style clothing of shorts and dresses. The children crowded around the white people.

Josh raised his hand in greeting as a village elder approached. 'Hola!'

The man nodded in return.

Josh pointed to the boat tied to the jetty. 'Me gustaria alquilar tu barco.'

Kirstin looked at Josh in astonishment. Was that Spanish he was talking?

'No es de alquiler, lo siento, no puedo ayudarte,' the elder said.

Josh took the elder by the arm and walked with him towards the jetty. As he went, Kirstin saw him pull a wad of bills from his pocket.

The children chattered excitedly. Naomi was holding her arms out and some children were stroking her bare skin.

'I don't think they see many white people here,' Kirstin said, and laughed.

'I so need to get a picture, they're so adorable,' Naomi said.

She pulled her mobile out and held it at arm's length to take a selfie. As many children as could crowded behind her and grinned widely at the lens. They've obviously done this before, Kirstin thought.

The bright flash illuminated the children's faces, and they giggled and blinked.

Naomi's mobile pinged with an alert.

'Did you just get a text message?' Kirstin said.

'Um, yeah,' Naomi said.

'Who's texting you out here?'

'Oh, no-one.'

Naomi tried to put her phone back in her pocket, but Kirstin grabbed her wrist and stopped her.

'Hold on, young lady. I don't like the look on your face.'

'Mum!'

'Who's texting you?'

Kirstin kept a firm but gentle hold of Naomi's wrist. She didn't want to get into a tug of war with her daughter over her phone, but Kirstin had the distinct feeling something was very wrong here.

'I told you, nobody important,' Naomi muttered.

'Give me your phone, let me see,' Kirstin said.

Naomi said nothing. She lowered her head.

'Naomi.'

Naomi gave her mother the phone.

Kirstin called up the message app. Her heart sank as she saw the messages.

'You've been texting Tyler?'

Naomi didn't say anything. The children had begun to grow bored and were wandering away.

'Naomi,' Kirstin said, suddenly finding it difficult to speak. 'Are you and Tyler in a relationship?'

'Maybe,' Naomi muttered quietly.

'And you've been messaging each other while we've been out here in the Amazon?'

Naomi nodded. Kirstin sighed heavily. 'I don't believe it, how could you?'

Naomi's head shot up as though it had been yanked on a string. 'Aren't I allowed a boyfriend?'

'But Julia's son? You've seen what she's like.'

'But Tyler's not like that, he's sweet and kind. And he hates his mum as much as you do.'

Josh arrived. 'Hey, we're good to go, we've got the boat.' He looked from Kirstin to Naomi and back again. 'What's wrong?'

Kirstin explained the situation.

'And you think that's how they've

been following you?' Josh said.

Kirstin nodded, her face grim. 'Naomi must have told Tyler where we were and he passed the information on.'

'No, Mum, I didn't.' Naomi was close to tears. 'You can read the messages, I never mentioned where we were, ever. And he never asked.'

'Charles wouldn't need Tyler to ask for that information,' Josh said. 'My guess he's been tracking you using the data signal from Naomi's phone every time she used it.'

Naomi suddenly threw herself at Kirstin, wrapping her arms around her mother's neck and sobbing, 'Oh, Mum! I'm so sorry!'

'It's alright,' Kirstin said, rubbing her hand over her daughter's back. 'It's not your fault.'

At least now Kirstin knew how Charles had been following her. But now he was the one in front, with the journal and her grandfather's map.

Kirstin couldn't help but smile, just a little. Charles didn't realise the map was missing some vital information. Which meant Kirstin might still have the upper hand.

9

The boat that Josh had paid good money for turned out to be not exactly seaworthy.

'This thing's got more holes in it than a sieve!' Josh shouted as he stared at the leaks springing up from the bottom of the boat.

They had been chugging upriver for about half an hour before Naomi spotted the first leak. Now there were five tiny fountains of water in various parts of the boat's hull, with more appearing every few minutes.

'What are we going to do?' Kirstin said, already standing in a puddle of water.

'There's not a lot we can do,' Josh replied, leaning on the throttle to squeeze as much power from the engine as he could. 'We've just got to keep going and hope that we catch up with your ex before we sink.'

Naomi held up the lantern that Josh

had also paid good money to the village elder for. Its light cast moving shadows across the boat's deck and the surface of the river. Kirstin flinched at a loud bang from behind, and Naomi screamed.

'It's just the engine backfiring,' Josh said. 'And now Charlie boy will have heard that for sure and he's going to know that someone is after him.'

'Do you think we should pull over to the side of the river soon?' Naomi said.

Kirstin looked down at the deck. They were up to their ankles in water now.

'You two need to start bailing water out,' Josh shouted.

'What with?' Kirstin shouted back. 'We haven't got anything to bail water out with.'

'Then use your hands!'

Kirstin turned to Naomi and said, 'We'd better do as he says'

Naomi nodded, eyes round and wide with fear.

Cupping their hands, they began bailing water out. Kirstin couldn't help but feel like King Canute ordering the tide to stop washing ashore. At least Canute was able to move his throne back up the beach when the waves began washing over his feet. In this leaky boat, the three of them had nowhere to go except down into the water.

Naomi screamed as something bumped against the side of the boat.

'What was that?' she yelled.

'I don't know,' Josh called back. 'Maybe a rock or something, just keep bailing.'

This is pointless, Kirstin thought. The water had risen to her shins. Bailing the water out of the boat with only their hands was having no effect at all. Another bump against the side of the boat had Naomi screaming again.

She lifted the lantern off the hook she had hung it from and leaned carefully over the side of the boat. She held the lantern up and its soft light illuminated the water. Kirstin saw her back stiffen. Naomi turned around, and if it was possible for Naomi's eyes to have grown even wider and rounder, then they had.

'What?' Kirstin said. 'What is it? What's wrong?'

'There's . . . there's . . . it's . . . um . . .'

'Naomi, just tell me, what did you see?'

'A crocodile!' Naomi blurted out. 'There's a huge crocodile in the river!'

Kirstin gripped the side of the boat. 'Josh, did you hear that?'

'Hear what?' Josh shouted over the howl of the engine.

'There are crocodiles in this river and we are sinking!'

'Alright, we're going in!'

'Thank goodness for that,' Kirstin said.

Another thump against the boat's hull trembled through Kirstin's feet and up her legs. The boat twisted in the water.

'What's that thing trying to do, sink us?' Josh yelled.

It doesn't need to try, Kirstin thought. We're already sinking. All that crocodile has to do is wait long enough and its supper will be delivered right into its waiting jaws.

'Let's start bailing the water out again,' Kirstin said to Naomi.

'But it's useless, Mum!' Naomi wailed. 'The water's rising too fast.'

'It's better than doing nothing,' Kirstin said, cupping her hands together and scooping water over the side of the boat. Naomi joined her.

As she bailed water, Kirstin looked at the riverbanks speeding by. The boat didn't seem to be moving any closer.

'Josh, are you headed in or what?' she shouted.

'I can see the others!' Josh shouted. 'I think we can catch them!'

I hope you know what you're doing, Kirstin thought.

Kirstin and Naomi continued frantically bailing out the water. It seemed to be rising faster than ever, and Kirstin didn't think they could make it to the riverbank now, anyway.

The crocodile hit the boat again, smashing it not once but twice. What was it doing, hitting them with its tail? The boat trembled and tilted to one side.

Because they were so low in the river, water gushed over the edge of the boat.

'We're sinking!' Naomi screamed.

The boat righted itself again, but there was far more water inside now.

Another thump, but this time it was Josh butting their sinking vessel up against Charles's boat. Oddball had already seen them and loomed over them, blocking their way on board. Kirstin grabbed the side of Charles's boat, holding on for dear life as the river's current tried to separate the two vessels.

Oddball raised a leg, ready to smash his booted foot down on Kirstin's hand.

'No!' Charles shouted. 'Let them on board!' The man lowered his leg and turned to look at his master. Kirstin helped Naomi climb on the boat first. The water was rushing around their knees now and they were sinking fast. Kirstin turned to call for Josh, but he was right behind her and helped her climb on Charles' boat before hauling himself aboard.

Just in time, as their boat disappeared

in a churning, boiling mass of water.

Wet, miserable and frightened, Kirstin could barely summon the energy to look up at Charles as he stood over her.

'My dear Kirstin, what have you been up to?'

'You almost got us killed!' Josh yelled, bunching his hands into fists.

Charles smiled. 'No, you almost got yourselves killed, but I saved your lives.'

'Why?' Kirstin said.

Charles regarded Kirstin silently. Julia had appeared by his side, and she looked contemptuously at Kirstin.

'I'm not sure,' Charles said, finally. 'Perhaps I care for you more than I realise . . .'

'You're not getting soft on me, are you Charles?' Julia said.

Naomi huddled up close to her mother. Josh still looked ready to fight, but Charles's man was keeping a careful watch on him.

'Never, my dear,' Charles said. 'But don't forget, Kirstin and I were married, even if only for a few hours.'

'All that time courting her, all that money spent on the wedding, and it was for nothing,' Julia said.

'What are you talking about?' Kirstin said, a worm of disquiet working its way through her chest and stomach.

Charles laughed. 'There you go again, you and your big mouth.'

'What are you talking about?' Kirstin repeated, more fiercely this time.

Julia squatted down in front of Kirstin, her eyes narrowed with hate. 'Charles only married you to help us find the Lost City of Quetzalcoatl.'

'Us?' Kirstin's chest filled with ice cold despair. 'You mean to say that you two plotted this together? That you already knew each other?'

Julia smiled, but it was far from pleasant. 'Charles and I have been lovers for many years. And it was me that told him all about grandfather's travels. The old fool confided in me once about the Lost City. I knew you would be the one to find out about it, one way or another. So I told Charles, and we hatched a plan for him to marry you. And then what was yours would be his.'

Kirstin's heart seemed to have shrivelled up inside her chest with despair. Despite hating Charles for his wedding day betrayal, she had still thought that he had loved her in his own way. At least a little. But now she could see that the courtship, the engagement and the wedding had all been a cold, calculated plan. Kirstin had been nothing more than a means to get what he wanted and once he had, Charles would have thrown her aside without a second thought.

'And you,' Julia sneered, turning her gaze on to Naomi. 'All those simpering, pathetic messages you've been sending Tyler have been so amusing. Tyler hasn't seen a single one of them.'

'But he's been replying to me, he — '

Tears welled up in Naomi's eyes.

'That's right,' Julia said, leaning in close to Naomi. 'All this time and you've been exchanging love messages with me. How very sweet.'

Naomi threw her hands over her face

and sobbed. Kirstin held her tight and glared at Julia.

'What are we going to do with them?' Julia said to Charles. 'You never should have allowed them on board, we should just throw them over the side now and have done with it.'

'Julia, you are such an evil monster, aren't you?' Charles said and chuckled. 'No, we'll let them stay with us for the moment. Besides, Julia's knowledge about the Lost City may well prove useful soon.'

10

'What's going on?' Josh said. 'First, he tried to kill us by sending us down the river to the waterfall and now he's letting us go with him?'

Kirstin finished taking a long swallow of water before she answered. The water was warm, but it still tasted good. Naomi had cuddled up next to her and her head lolled on her chest as she dozed, despite the steady puttering of the boat's engine. Charles had allowed Kirstin and Naomi to have their rucksacks back, and Kirstin clung to hers like it was a lifesaver.

'Charles has realised he hasn't got all the information he needs,' Kirstin replied.

Josh glanced at Dewberry, standing in the cabin. 'He's got the map, hasn't he?'

'Yes, but the map's not complete, look I'll show you.' Kirstin opened her rucksack and pulled out a creased and stained sheet of paper.

'What's that?' Josh said as he leaned in close.

'It's a photocopy of the map from my grandfather's journal.' Kirstin unfolded the sheet of paper. 'Look, this is the river.' She pointed at a scrawled line. 'And we're headed up it.' She traced the route with her finger.

'And where's this lost city you're all so fascinated by?'

'Here.' Kirstin pointed at an X drawn on the other half of the sheet of paper.

'But there's no map on this side,' Josh said. 'The paper's blank.'

'Exactly. X marks the spot, but Walter never finished drawing the map, so we don't know where the X points to.'

Josh took the sheet of paper off Kirstin and examined it. 'But that doesn't make any sense. How is anybody expected to find this city if they only have half a map?'

'Because there's another clue, another part of the map waiting for us when we get to where this map ends, I'm sure of it,' Kirstin said.

Josh glanced up at Dewberry who was still in the cabin with Moses. 'And he doesn't know where that is, does he?'

Julia grinned and shook her head.

'But you do, right?'

Julia stopped smiling and shook her head again.

'Are you kidding me?' Josh hissed. 'I thought you knew the way to this lost city.'

Naomi stirred, and muttered, 'If we knew the way it wouldn't be lost, would it?'

'Smart Alec,' Josh muttered.

Her eyes still closed, Naomi smiled.

'Julia said that Grandfather told her he almost found the Lost City, but I don't think he was telling her the truth. I think he did find it.'

'But if that's the case, why did he never say anything?' Josh said. 'And you read all his journals, wouldn't he have written about it at least?'

'I think he did. After reading all his journals I realised there has to be one missing. Grandfather dated all his entries, and there's a period of about six months that I can't account for.'

'So what do you think happened to that one?'

'I think Granddad hid or destroyed the journal with details of the Lost City in it. I think he decided it should stay lost, for whatever reason.'

'But what about the map? Why didn't he destroy that?'

Kirstin thought for a moment. 'I'm not sure. Maybe he couldn't bear to completely destroy all his evidence that it exists. And maybe that's why we only have half a map, because he didn't want to make it too easy for anybody else to find it.'

Josh sat back and blew out his cheeks in frustration. 'I don't know, it all sounds a little crazy to me.'

'Maybe, but I think we can find the next clue,' Kirstin said. 'But we have to be careful, we can't let Charles and Julia know. They mustn't find the Lost City.'

Moses was steering them into the river bank. Josh took Kirstin's hand and gave it a quick, reassuring squeeze. Kirstin gave him a brief smile in return. Despite all his bravado, Kirstin found she was growing to like him.

'On your feet!' Dewberry commanded. 'We walk from now on.'

Kirstin roused herself from her thoughts and helped Naomi to her feet.

'Put on your backpacks,' Dewberry said.

The night sky was tinged with blue and the stars had begun to fade away as the rising sun brought daylight. A massive tree had fallen across the river and blocked the way. Kirstin's grandfather had marked the tree's position on his hand-drawn map. The river was wide and deep here, and only the riverbank on their right-hand side was accessible. But they needed to be on the opposite bank.

Kirstin's grandfather had indicated with a dotted line on the map that they needed to cross the river on the fallen tree trunk. The group gathered up their belongings and hefted rucksacks onto their backs. Josh got handed a spare rucksack to carry. Oddball carried the largest backpack. Kirstin thought it might be a tent.

They had to climb over the edge of the boat and jump onto the muddy river bank. Moses jumped off the side and landed with a squelch in the mud. He turned his back on Kirstin and Josh. It seemed he couldn't bear to look them in the eye.

'Let's fill our canteens up,' Dewberry said. 'We have a long walk ahead of us.'

Kirstin and Josh knelt down by the river and dipped their canteens in the water. The canteens had special water purifying filters inside them. As Kirstin held her canteen in the water she noticed tiny disturbances on the river's surface.

'It looks like there are fish in this river,' she said and pointed.

'We'd best be careful,' Josh replied, lifting his canteen from the water. 'We've no idea what lives in this water.'

Kirstin lifted her canteen out too. It was full anyway.

They straightened up and stepped back from the riverbank. Kirstin lifted her face to the sunlight just breaking over the tops of the trees.

'Enjoy it,' Josh said. 'Once we get into the heart of the rainforest, you won't see much of the sun at all.'

'Is the forest really that dense and heavy?' she asked him.

'More than you think,' Josh replied.

A scream cut through the air. Startled, a flock of birds burst from a tree and flew into the sky.

Moses, kneeling on the riverbank, snatched his hand from the water and screamed again. Blood poured from his hand.

And, Kirstin realised with a sudden shock, he was missing a finger. Josh and Dewberry both dashed over to Moses and hauled him away from the river's edge. Moses sobbed and wailed.

'We need a tourniquet,' Josh said. 'We need to stop the bleeding.'

Dewberry pulled a first aid kit from his rucksack and found a roll of bandage.

He unrolled a length and swiftly wrapped it around the stump of Moses' finger and pulled it tight until the blood stopped flowing. Josh applied some antiseptic and then dressed the wound. Moses had stopped wailing and instead was crying quietly.

'We need to get him back, find a doctor,' Josh said.

Dewberry shook his head. 'No, we carry on.'

'Don't be ridiculous!' Josh snapped. 'This trip isn't worth a man's life. If we don't get him medical help, then this wound will get infected and depending on how soon he gets medical treatment after that will mean the difference between him losing that hand or losing his life.'

Dewberry stood up. 'He will be fine, won't you Moses?'

Moses wiped at his eyes with his sleeve and nodded. Flies buzzed around his face and his bandaged hand. Josh made his way back across the mud to Kirstin and Naomi. 'This is stupid. Moses will die if we don't get him medical help.'

'What happened?' Kirstin said. 'Was it that crocodile?'

Josh shook his head, his face grim. 'No, it looks like this section of the river is infested with piranhas. That's all that could have taken Moses' finger off like that.'

Dewberry helped Moses away from the river's edge. Moses looked pale, and he was sweating profusely.

'Keep that thing away from me,' Julia said, staring at the bandaged hand which was already turning a bright red.

'As usual my cousin is full of sympathy for her fellow man,' Kirstin muttered.

Charles led the way with the map in the journal and a handheld GPS Wayfinder. As they walked, Charles' manservant hacked at the undergrowth with a scythe and cleared a path. They pushed their way through the thick, unyielding forest until they reached the roots of the massive tree that lay across the river. A crude rope ladder had been hung from it.

The manservant climbed the rope

ladder first, hauling himself up until he was standing on the horizontal tree trunk. Moses went next and this time Josh was allowed to help him. Josh followed Moses and soon they were all gathered at the base of the tree. Kirstin looked out across the river to the opposite bank. All they had to do now was walk across this improvised bridge. And hope they didn't slip and fall into the river full of piranha fish. Great.

The tree trunk was thick and wide, but gnarled with stubby, broken branches and knots. New life had sprung up in much of the bark between the gaps. This was going to be more like an obstacle course than a path to the other side of the river. Not too difficult for most of the group, but how would Moses manage? He now only had the use of one hand, and he still looked as though he might faint at any moment.

'Moses, you go first,' Dewberry said.

'Let me go with him and help,' Josh said.

'No,' Dewberry replied.

'Come on, look at him!' Josh took a step toward Dewberry but the manservant blocked his path with one large hand on Josh's chest. 'He's going to slip and fall in the river unless someone goes with him and helps him.'

'We'll be right behind you,' Dewberry said to Moses. 'There's nothing to worry about, off you go.'

With one fearful glance at the water below, Moses began inching along the tree trunk. Using his uninjured hand, he gripped onto the branches jutting towards the sky like bony fingers.

Kirstin and Josh looked at each other, but said nothing.

'Mum?' Naomi said.

Kirstin took her hand. 'Don't worry, just walk slowly and carefully and you'll be fine.'

Dewberry started crossing the tree trunk next, followed by Julia. Josh nodded to indicate that Kirstin and Naomi should follow on. Kirstin looked back at the manservant, standing passively and waiting for everyone to get moving. It looked like Dewberry had told him to follow on behind everyone else.

'We'll cross together,' Kirstin said to her daughter. 'You go in front, and like I said, take your time and use the branches to hold on to.'

Naomi nodded. She began taking hesitant steps along the tree's thick, gnarled trunk. Kirstin followed her, keeping up close so that she could steady her daughter if she slipped.

Soon they were over the river. Kirstin looked up at the densely packed trees on the opposite bank. All she had to do was keep walking, keep moving forward toward the safety of the ground on the opposite side of the river.

Seeing that Naomi was making steady progress, Kirstin glanced back over her shoulder. Josh wasn't too far behind, and Oddball was directly behind him. They were all on the tree trunk now, over the river. Kirstin craned her neck and saw Moses up ahead, climbing gingerly down off the tree trunk and onto the ground. Julia jumped down after him.

Josh cried out. Kirstin whipped round, almost losing her footing but managing to steady herself.

'Josh!' she yelled.

Josh was hanging from the tree trunk, his arms stretched out. His feet dangled in the water up to his ankles. What had happened? Had he slipped? Or had Charles's manservant pushed him?

'Lift your feet out of the river!' Kirstin shouted.

Josh bent his knees and his feet rose from out of the water. The manservant stood silently on the tree trunk, observing Josh but doing nothing to help him. Josh pulled himself up, the tendons in his neck standing out with the effort.

'Don't just stand there doing nothing, help him!' Kirstin yelled at the manservant.

Oddball simply stared back at Kirstin, his face a blank mask.

'Charles!' Kirstin yelled. 'Tell that freak of yours to help Josh!'

Dewberry rolled his eyes. 'Oh, Kirstin, why on earth should I do that?'

'Because you need me to find the Lost City of Quetzalcoatl, that's why,' she hissed. 'And if you allow Josh to fall into that river then I will never help you.'

'Do you really think you have any choice in that?' Charles said, his voice low and menacing.

'Don't test me, Charles,' Kirstin replied.

Charles regarded her for a few more moments, his eyes hooded and blank. Finally he lifted his head and shouted, 'Oddball, help the flyboy up would you, there's a good chap.'

The huge, silent man bent down and fastened a massive hand around Josh's wrist and lifted him like a doll. Josh scrambled for footing amongst the branches as he rose. Once he was back on the trunk and the manservant had released him, Josh clung onto the gnarled branches.

He turned on the manservant. 'You pushed me!' The big man gazed back at Josh, his face a blank.

'He pushed me,' Josh said, turning to Kirstin.

'Let's get on to the ground,' Kirstin said, silently pleading with him to calm down. His face set in a scowl, Josh nodded.

Kirstin headed for the riverbank again. Naomi had made it and she was standing with the others.

Had Charles' manservant pushed Josh off the trunk? After all, Charles didn't need him, in fact he was extra baggage, and troublesome baggage at that. Charles needed Kirstin on this expedition, but only Kirstin. Josh was extra baggage, a nuisance to be put up with. But was Charles really prepared to kill Josh?

And Kirstin might have made a deal with Charles for the moment to keep Josh alive, but how long would that last?

Another thought struck Kirstin, sending chills down her spine.

Josh wasn't the only member of this group Charles could do without.

Wasn't Naomi extra baggage too?

11

They tramped through the rainforest for the rest of the day. Using the map and his GPS, Charles led the group through the forest, only occasionally consulting with Kirstin on the route they should take. He seemed to be possessed in his determination to find the Lost City, and that obsession was growing as he drew closer.

Kirstin couldn't help but wonder what he would do with his captives once he had found what he wanted. All three of them would be extra baggage at that point, and Kirstin no longer had any illusions that Charles might have cared for her once. Both he and Julia had been revealed to be scheming and heartless.

How could Kirstin have been taken in by Charles's charms? Despite the heat, she shuddered. To think she had almost let that monster into their family. Naomi had seen through him. She hadn't seen the whole picture, the true extent of his wickedness, but she had seen him for what he was.

Kirstin wondered if she was fit to be a mother. It seemed she had got into the habit of placing her daughter in danger, first through the marriage and now here, in the Amazon.

Maybe when they got back to England, she should have a long, hard think about her priorities.

If they got back.

Kirstin's thoughts turned to Josh. Knowing that he had once been married to Julia, Kirstin could understand why he had relocated out here as far away from other people as he could get. Kirstin could sense the barriers that he held up between him and everybody else. He was abrupt and rude, but Kirstin could still detect a sensitive, lovely nature beneath all his bluster. Trust Julia to turn him into a lonely, cynical hermit.

Between them Julia and Charles had managed to ruin not only Kirstin's life, but Josh's too.

Charles called everyone to a stop.

'Where now, Kirstin?' he called out.

'How am I supposed to know?' Kirstin muttered. 'You've got the same information as me.'

Josh placed a gentle hand on her shoulder. 'Don't get him angry.'

'Get over here!' Julia snapped and grabbed Kirstin by the wrist and dragged her to where Charles stood examining the hand-drawn map.

Kirstin pulled herself free and glared at her cousin. 'Keep your hands off me from now on!'

'Yeah? Or what?'

'Ladies, ladies, please,' Charles said. 'Retract your claws and save your cat fight until after we have reached our destination.'

Kirstin and Julia glared at each other. There was no way that Kirstin was going to be the first to break eye contact.

'Come, come,' Charles said, taking Julia by the shoulders and turning her away. 'Please go and check on Moses, I suspect he is not well.'

Kirstin's spirits revived a little as Julia was made to break eye contact first. Childish, Kirstin knew, but still satisfying.

Charles held out the journal, open at the hand-drawn map. He stabbed a finger at the X.

'Here we are, and yet I see no sign that we have reached our destination.' Charles looked from the map to Kirstin, his eyes narrowing. 'What do you say?'

'The site of the Lost City is over here,' Kirstin replied, pointing at the second X, in the middle of the blank space on the paper.

'And how do we get there?' Charles said, his voice soft and yet full of menace.

'I don't know,' Kirstin said. 'But my grandfather wanted us to get here first, otherwise why would he have marked the spot on the map?'

'So you think this place is important?'

'Yes, I do, but I don't know why.'

Charles continued to stare at Kirstin, his eyes narrowing. 'Alright everyone, let's spread out and search this area. There must be something here to point us in the right direction.'

The area that Charles was talking about was dense with foliage and trees. Hanging vines snagged at Kirstin's hair and face, and she tripped over roots and creeping tendrils snaking across the ground. Naomi stayed close by Kirstin's side. Charles's manservant shadowed Josh wherever he went. Josh threw hostile stares at him, but it made no difference.

Why had Kirstin's grandfather marked this spot on his map? There was nothing that Kirstin could see that might help them onto the next stage of their journey. Perhaps they had all misunderstood the map, or his intentions in drawing it. Maybe there wasn't even a Lost City, that it was a myth. After all, how could an entire city, even an ancient one, avoid satellite detection unless it was buried and hidden from view?

They continued their search, spreading wider and further, until Charles called them all back.

'This is pointless, there is nothing here of any use to us,' he said. 'Perhaps the old fool simply never finished drawing his silly little map, and here we are acting like bigger fools than he was thinking we can find a clue to help us on our way.'

Kirstin had an uneasy feeling that he might be right. Maybe the X in the blank space of the page referred to nothing. Disappointment churned in Kirstin's stomach. Despite everything, despite the danger and the betrayal, disappointment was still the overriding emotion.

The canopy of leaves above their heads began hissing as another shower began. Seconds later and rainwater was pouring off the trees and drenching Kirstin and the rest of the group.

'We should try and find some shelter,' Josh said. 'This might turn into a heavy downfall.'

As if to prove Josh correct, the rainfall switched to a deluge. The ground turned into mud, heavy raindrops splattering mud against Kirstin's boots.

Over the noise of the rain hitting the

leaves and then the ground, Kirstin thought she heard something else.

Something like . . . like a drum.

'Can you hear that?' she shouted, strands of her hair plastered against her face.

'Hear what?' Charles shouted back.

'That noise, that . . . drumming.'

She felt stupid for saying it, but Josh cocked his head and listened.

'Yes, I can hear it,' he said, pointing to his left. 'It's coming from over there.'

Josh started walking in the direction of the sound and Kirstin, holding Naomi's hand, followed him. He stopped in a small clearing, cocked his head to one side again and listened some more. The drumming sound was louder. In fact, it sounded as though it was coming from beneath their feet.

'Have we got anything to dig with?' Josh had to shout to be heard over the torrential downpour.

'No!' Dewberry shouted back.

'Then we'll have to dig with our hands!' Josh yelled. He got down on his

145

knees and began digging his hands into the dirt, pulling at the creepers and the foliage.

Charles ordered his manservant to join Josh and dig. Kirstin knelt down beside Josh. 'Are you sure you know what you're doing? How deep are you intending to go?'

'Not very deep at all,' Josh said and grinned.

Kirstin looked down, expecting to see the ground, but instead saw a wooden board.

'This is why we can hear that hollow drumming sound.' Josh cleared more mud off the board to reveal another attached to it. 'Someone's been here before and dug a hole and then covered it over with these wooden panels.'

Granddad, thought Kirstin.

With renewed energy they started clearing the mud and the undergrowth off the board. Charles's manservant helped them. The others stood and watched, rain running down their faces.

'Hey, I've found the edge!' Kirstin

shouted.

Josh joined her and they dug away at the mud, revealing a hard lip in the ground. Josh traced along with his fingers, digging away at the mud until he reached a corner. With the three of them working together they were able to clear enough mud away to reveal an oblong wooden trapdoor in the ground, with a large iron handle.

'What on earth is down there?' Josh said.

'Um, has anyone else noticed that it looks about the length and width of a body?' Naomi said. 'Like a coffin?'

'Open it up,' Dewberry said.

Kirstin stood up. 'How about you open it up? Get your hands dirty for once.'

Dewberry's lip curled back in a sneer. 'My hands are dirty enough, thank you Kirstin. You should know that.'

The rain stopped, as though somebody had simply turned it off. For a second there was complete silence, and then the forest erupted into a cacophony of squawks, screeches and animal calls.

Kirstin wiped rainwater off her face. She was tired, hungry and dirty and she just wanted to go home. Even without finding the Lost City.

Oddball squatted beside the trapdoor and pulled the iron ring. Nothing happened.

The manservant tried again, this time leaning back and hauling at the iron ring. The trapdoor shifted slightly. Planting his feet wider apart, he hauled at the wooden panelling. The whole thing came loose. Kirstin had expected it to open on hinges, but it didn't. Instead the panel of wood was dragged away by the manservant to reveal a dark hole in the ground.

'Look at the sides of the hole,' Josh said.

Kirstin looked. 'What about them?'

'They're perfectly straight,' Josh replied. 'Whoever dug this hole made a remarkably neat job of it.'

'What's down there?' Dewberry said. Neither he nor Julia had made any attempt to draw closer.

Josh and Kirstin both peered into the

hole.

'I don't know, it's too dark to see,' Kirstin said. Dewberry finally stepped closer. He pulled a torch from his rucksack, pointed it into the oblong hole in the ground and flicked on the light.

Naomi screamed. At the bottom of the deep hole lay a human skeleton, over which scurried a dark mass of insects.

Kirstin wrapped her arm around Naomi's shoulders and hugged her close.

Josh bent down, placing his hands on his knees. 'Look, is he holding something in his hands?'

Dewberry shone the torch onto the skeleton's hands, resting on its ribcage. 'What is that?'

'I don't know, it looks almost like a sheet of paper, but that can't be right,' Josh said. 'Paper wouldn't survive anytime at all in these conditions.'

'Perhaps you should climb down there and have a closer look,' Julia said.

Kirstin clenched her teeth and bit back a sarcastic response.

'That sounds like a good idea, darling,' Dewberry said, gazing at Josh and grinning.

'Be my guest.' Josh held out his hand, as if to say, After you.

Dewberry chuckled. 'Oh no, I don't think so.'

Dewberry ordered his manservant to unpack the rucksack and retrieve the rope. He tied the rope around a massive tree trunk and fed it out across the mud until it reached the hole.

Charles's manservant held out the end of the rope to Josh.

'Tie it around your waist,' Dewberry said.

Josh laughed, although there was no humour in it. 'Are you kidding me? You think I'm going to let you lower me down there so that you can put the door back in place and leave me to starve to death?'

'Really, Mr Hanson, you're not thinking straight, are you?' Dewberry replied. 'Why would I leave you down there when I want you to go and retrieve whatever it is our malnourished friend is clutching between his bony fingers?'

'I don't know, but I'm sure you could find a reason.'

Josh glanced into the pit and then at Kirstin.

She could see from the expression on his face that he was tempted, despite the very real danger. He wanted to know what the skeleton was clutching to its ribcage too. But he didn't want to be imprisoned down there either.

'Now come on, Mr Hanson, let's not be silly about this. We all know you're going to do as I say. You wouldn't want any trouble, would you?'

'We could always send the brat down, instead,' Julia said, grabbing Naomi by the arm.

Kirstin lashed out, grabbing a fistful of Julia's hair and yanking her head back hard and fast. Julia screamed and let go of Naomi.

'Take your hands off me!' Julia yelled.

Julia threw herself at Kirstin and they both slammed into the muddy ground. Kirstin landed on her back on a gnarly root sticking out of the ground. The impact winded her. As she struggled to catch her breath, a white hot pain shot through her scalp. She was being dragged by her hair!

Kirstin lifted her hands and found Julia's wrists. Julia let go of Kirstin's hair and pulled her arms free. Before Kirstin could react, she felt the sharp dig of a boot in her side.

She rolled over from the impact and found the ground dropping away from beneath her.

'Kirstin!' she heard Josh yell as she plummeted into the pit.

12

Kirstin hit the ground hard, the impact knocking the breath from her lungs. The skeleton shattered beneath her when she landed on it, the snapping sounds of breaking bones filling her head. For a moment she lay there, stunned. She was on her back and she could see the oblong opening above her, like a window onto another world that she had just left.

The oblong window filled with heads, worried faces looking down at her.

'Kirstin?' Josh called.

'Mum?'

'I'm alright,' Kirstin said. That wasn't quite true, or at least she wasn't entirely sure if it was true just yet. She hadn't tried moving, she didn't know if she had suffered any broken bones.

She rotated her head. Okay, that felt fine. A little stiff, but the movement had been free of pain. Just a little tickle at the back of her neck. She tried lifting an arm, and then the other one. Both arms worked fine. That itch on the back of her neck was getting worse, though. And there were more, on her shoulders, her back, down her legs.

Kirstin's body stiffened as she remembered seeing all the insects scurrying over the skeleton. With a scream she hauled herself upright, forgetting about checking for any injuries first.

'What's wrong?' Josh yelled.

Somebody up above had found the torch, and the light spilled into the deep grave and illuminated the shattered skeleton and the crawling cockroaches. Their black bodies glistened in the torchlight as they scuttled over the bones. So many of them, a seething black carpet. And they were on Kirstin too. In her hair, dropping from her body and her arms and legs, and swarming over her feet.

'Cockroaches!' she screamed.

Kirstin bent her head and shook it, running her fingers through her hair to dislodge the enormous insects. Their tiny legs tickled against her scalp and her hands as she swiped at them. She lifted a foot out of the mass of scurrying bodies and kicked the roaches off. But there was nowhere to stand, nowhere to put her foot back down again, except back on the insects.

When she placed her foot back down, Kirstin screamed again as she heard the insect bodies pop beneath the force of her boot.

'What's wrong?' Josh shouted.

'Will you stop asking me that?' Kirstin screamed. 'I've told you what's wrong!'

'But you keep screaming!'

'Just get me out of here!' Kirstin yelled.

So many of them, crawling up her legs, more of them still on her torso and her arms, and in her hair. And they were so big.

Could they bite? Were they poisonous?

And the stink. Kirstin gagged. How could she even breathe down here?

A length of rope fell on her head, dislodging more black insects.

'Tie the rope around your waist and we'll pull you up!' Josh shouted.

'Wait!' That was Charles's voice. 'The thing the skeleton was holding, can you see it?'

'You have got to be kidding me!' Kirstin grabbed the rope and tied it around her waist. 'Okay, I'm ready, get me out of here.'

'No.' Charles again. Kirstin looked up and saw him peering down at her. 'You need to find whatever it was that the skeleton was holding. It is important.'

'How about you come down and look for it yourself?' Kirstin yelled. 'Just pull me out of here.'

'No. Not until you have found it.'

Kirstin screamed in frustration and anger. She looked down at the cockroaches and shuddered. The shattered skeleton had almost disappeared beneath the insects. The effect of their mass was like the surface of a black sea undulating across the shattered bones.

And she saw it. What they had thought was a sheet of paper stuck up out of the swirling mass of cockroaches. It couldn't be paper, it was too strong. Kirstin bent down to take a closer look, but it disappeared beneath the heaving carpet of roaches as they clambered over each other.

Kirstin straightened up. To retrieve the mysterious object, Kirstin would have to plunge her hand into the mass of cockroaches. No way. She couldn't do that. Those things were revolting.

But if she didn't, her cheating, manipulating, scheming ex would keep her down here.

Kirstin sucked in a deep breath of stinking air and let it out in a howl of anger and defiance. At the same time she plunged her hand into the scuttling, scurrying cockroaches. Her fingers closed around the object and she pulled it clear.

'I've got it!' she yelled. 'Pull me up now!'

The rope pulled taut and then she was lifted off the seething carpet of insects. Kirstin steadied herself against the dirt wall as Oddball pulled her up out of the pit in jerky, halting stages. When she reached the lip of the hole, she hauled herself over the edge, hands grabbing her by the arms and helping her out.

Kirstin stood up, her limbs trembling and aching. Charles approached her. 'Did you get it? Where is it?'

Kirstin raised her hand and slapped him hard across the face. He raised his hand to his cheek, already turning red, and stared at Kirstin. 'I suppose I deserved that.'

'Oh, you deserve far more than that!' Kirstin snarled.

She raised her arm again, but Josh grabbed her and pulled her away.

'I know, I know,' he whispered as Kirstin struggled to free herself from his enveloping grip. 'Save it, all that anger, store it up, okay? There's nothing we can do right now, but his time will come, it will.'

Kirstin relaxed and Josh let her go.

Josh picked up the object Kirstin had brought up with her from where it had dropped on the ground. The others crowded closer.

'What is it?' Julia said.

The object was thin and square, just like a sheet of paper. But it was made of tin. It was bent slightly from where Kirstin had landed on it, and it had a series of thin, spidery lines cut into it.

'Have you any idea?' Josh said, handing the tin plate to Kirstin. She held it up at arm's length and squinted at it.

'I think,' she said, speaking slowly, 'I think it's a map.'

'It's the other half of the map, showing us the way to the Lost City!' Dewberry exclaimed.

He pulled the journal out of a pocket and opened it up.

'Turn around!' he snapped at his manservant.

The big man did as he was told and Dewberry laid the journal against the man's back.

Kirstin, forgetting all about the cockroaches as her excitement grew, placed the tin plate over the blank half of the paper. The lines at the edge of the map in the journal and the lines cut into the tin plate met at the joining edge.

'Has anyone got a pen or a pencil?' Kirstin said.

'Here.' Dewberry handed Kirstin his ornate, gold pen that looked like it might have cost more than Kirstin earned in a month.

She traced along the lines cut out of the tin plate. There were many of them, some of them quite intricate, and drawing onto the manservant's back wasn't the easiest thing to do. But finally she finished. She took the square piece of tin off the page and stepped back.

Everyone crowded in to have a look.

'Darling, you were right, it's the rest of the map,' Julia whispered.

★ ★ ★

Josh helped Kirstin clean up and find any remaining cockroaches still trapped in her hair and her clothes. He brushed through her long hair with his fingers, flicking away any cockroaches he found. Kirstin liked the attention. It almost made falling into a pit full of cockroaches and landing on a skeleton worthwhile.

'Who do you think that dead guy down there is?' Josh said.

They were sitting on a large rock with Naomi. As a group they had decided to settle down for the night and move on in the morning, but they had split into two camps. Dewberry and Julia, with the manservant and Moses, had picked another spot just out of sight behind some trees. Kirstin was relieved to have some respite from their presence. Having to be around Charles and Julia all the time was exhausting.

'I don't know,' Kirstin replied thoughtfully.

'Maybe he was a friend of great-granddad's and he died,' Naomi said.

'Or,' Kirstin said, thinking back to the day her father showed her the trunk with her granddad's journals in, 'maybe that is your great-granddad's brother, Edwin.'

'The one that went missing?' Josh said.

'Do you think Walter buried him there?' Naomi gasped.

'But why?' Josh said. 'That's a very deep hole to be buried in, and why cover the hole with a plank instead of filling it with earth?'

'And why leave that tin map in his hands as well?'

Kirstin held up her hands. 'Hold on, that's just too many questions for my tired brain to think about answering.'

Josh finished running his fingers through Kirstin's hair. 'There, I think that's all of them.'

Kirstin sighed with relief. 'Thank you so much. It was actually quite relaxing as well.'

Josh grinned. 'My pleasure. Anytime you have need of my services, just give me a call.'

Kirstin gazed into his eyes for a moment or two. 'I might just do that.'

Naomi stretched. 'I think I'm going to go to bed, I'm exhausted.'

'That's a good idea, we should all get some sleep,' Josh said.

They made their beds on the shelf of rock and lay down. Kirstin thought it would take her ages to get to sleep, but she fell into a deep slumber almost immediately and slept through the night.

When they awoke in the morning, they found they were on their own.

The others had left without them.

13

'They obviously decided they don't need us anymore,' Josh said.

Kirstin sat at the edge of the pit, looking down at the cockroaches and the shattered skeleton. She sighed heavily.

'What do you think we should do now?' she asked, eventually.

'Might be an idea to head back, return to that village where we hired the boat,' Josh said. 'I reckon we've got enough food and water to get us back there, at least.'

'But what about Charles and Julia?' Naomi said. 'We can't let them find the Lost City of Quetzalcoatl.'

'What chance do we have of finding it now?' Josh replied. 'I can't even pronounce it, let alone find it, and we don't even have a map anymore.'

Kirstin said nothing, just kept gazing down into the pit.

'Can't you track them through the

forest?' Naomi said.

Josh laughed. 'Do I look like Grizzly Adams? I'm a pilot, not an Indian tracker.'

Naomi folded her arms and scowled. 'We have to do something.'

Kirstin roused herself and stood up. 'Joshua is right, we should head back. I've put you in enough danger on this trip.'

Naomi's scowl deepened. 'It's not fair.'

'I know,' Josh said, gently. 'But life's not fair. And that's something you're just going to have to get used to. The thing is though, you've got people who love you and care for you. Charles and Julia? They've got nothing but hate and selfishness.'

Kirstin looked at Josh and her heart filled with tenderness. 'What a lovely thing to say.'

'Yeah, underneath this hard-bitten, cynical exterior lurks a heart of . . . well, I'm not sure what exactly, but maybe something approaching decent humanity.'

'Alright you two, cut it out,' Naomi snapped. 'I still say we should follow the others. They can't have got far.'

'And what do we do if we catch up with them?' Josh said. 'Ask them if we can pretty please join them on their adventure?'

Naomi's scowl deepened even more. 'There you go, being all smart-mouthed again.'

'But he's right,' Kirstin said. 'We're heading back, and that's all there is to it. Let's get moving.'

Josh picked up Kirstin's rucksack and slung it over his shoulder. Kirstin picked up Naomi's lighter rucksack.

Naomi remained seated on the ground.

Kirstin pulled the photocopy of the map from a side pocket in the rucksack and unfolded it. She looked at it thoughtfully.

'What?' Josh said. 'Why are you looking at that?'

'Just thinking,' Kirstin replied.

'Thinking about what? You're missing half the map, we need to turn around and head back. What is there to think about?'

Kirstin turned the sheet of paper around and showed it to Josh. 'I copied the other half of the map onto the photocopy last night.'

Naomi jumped to her feet. 'Does that mean we're going to find the Lost City?'

'Uh-uh, no way!' Josh sliced his hand through the air in a chopping motion. 'Forget about it, it's far too dangerous. You've seen what those two are capable of. If we follow them, we could die out here.'

Naomi hopped from foot to foot. 'Mum?'

Kirstin sighed. After everything she had said about how she had been foolhardy and selfish to put Naomi in danger, and now she was considering it again. Would she ever learn? And yet . . .

'If you do this, I'm headed back,' Josh said. 'I'm not going to be a part of this.'

'You wouldn't do that,' Kirstin replied.

'You don't think so?'

'Leave two defenceless women all alone in the rainforest? No, I don't think you would.'

Josh scowled. 'Yeah? Well, just watch me.' He pulled Kirstin's rucksack off his back and let it fall to the ground. 'Have a nice life.'

He turned and began walking away. Kirstin watched him. After walking a few paces, Josh stopped and turned back.

'Are you seriously doing this?' he yelled. 'I mean, seriously?'

Kirstin turned to Naomi. 'What do you think?'

'You know what I think. We should go, we're wasting time.'

'Your granddad will be furious with me when he finds out.'

Naomi smiled. 'Maybe, but what about your granddad?'

'He would have been cross too.'

'But a little disappointed too, don't you think?'

Kirstin nodded slowly. 'Yeah, a little disappointed too.'

Naomi's grin widened.

Kirstin turned back to Josh. 'When you get back to the village, would you mind waiting for us there?'

'You're serious about this, aren't you?' he said.

'Yep.'

'And there's nothing I can do to change your mind?'

'Nope.'

Josh sighed, threw his arms in the air and walked back to Kirstin and Naomi. 'I'm about as crazy as you two.'

★ ★ ★

The map took them back to the river which had now transformed into a series of rapids. Even if they'd had a boat, they couldn't have used it now. There would have been no choice but to continue on foot. Behind the mountains, dark clouds were forming.

'Looks like we might have some bad weather coming our way,' Josh said.

'Worse than we've already had?' Kirstin said.

Josh scrunched his forehead up in thought. 'I'd say so, yes. That looks like a nasty storm front. If we're lucky, it will miss us completely.' 'But if it's headed our way?' Kirstin said.

'We'll be in trouble.'

They continued walking. The water cascaded over the rocky shelves on their left and to their right the forest dropped away dramatically. Their route along the side of the river was narrow, rocky, and steep. The tops of Kirstin's thighs ached with the effort of the climb, and she could feel the pressure on her knees. Every inch of her body dripped with sweat and the rucksack's straps had begun to dig into her shoulders.

And yet, somehow, she was happy. She was doing what she loved the most; exploring. And she was with her daughter and Josh. Kirstin's stomach performed a little somersault. Why did it matter that Josh was with her? Why should that make her happy? Because she felt safe having him around? Or was there more to it than that?

Kirstin could hardly believe he had once been married to Julia. It was difficult to picture the two of them together. That had to have been one fiery relationship. Kirstin's lips twitched with a little smile of amusement at that thought.

'What's so funny?' Josh said.

'Oh, nothing,' Kirstin replied.

'Huh,' Josh grunted. 'Somehow I have the distinct feeling that you're laughing at me.'

'And just why would I be laughing at you?' Kirstin said.

'I don't know, but I'm thinking there's something going on here that I don't know about.'

'You're just paranoid, that's all.'

'Can you blame me? I was married to your cousin for six whole months.'

Kirstin burst out laughing. 'That long? I'm impressed. How did you manage it?'

'It wasn't easy, I can tell you. Being married to Julia was like climbing this trail every day, all alone and blindfolded and carrying a rucksack full of fireworks on your back and hoping that nobody had lit the fuse.'

'That bad, huh?'

Josh looked sideways at Kirstin. 'Honestly? No, it was worse.'

Kirstin started laughing again. It felt good. Seemed like she hadn't laughed in a long time.

'Well, I'm glad you find it amusing,' Josh said, but he was smiling and his eyes were alive with good humour.

'I'm sorry!' Kirstin gasped, trying to control the urge to laugh again. 'But I think you managed to describe my cousin perfectly. At least you could divorce her, I still have to call her family.'

A shadow seemed to pass over Josh's face and his smile faltered. 'To be honest, I didn't want to divorce her. I'm kind of old-fashioned like that and I was prepared to work through whatever we needed to. Being married to Julia was exactly how I just described it, but when we first met, it wasn't like that. At first I thought all the fireworks were because we'd married too quickly, you know, we hadn't given ourselves time to get to know each other properly. But there we were, man and wife, and I wasn't about to throw that away on account of us having rushed into it.'

'And then you came home that one day and found her with another man?' Kirstin said, thinking back to what Josh had said yesterday.

Naomi was standing beside Kirstin and slipped her hand into her mother's. She could obviously tell that Josh was in a vulnerable place, and she didn't want to break the moment by speaking.

Josh sighed. 'No, not quite, that wasn't the end of it. We argued, we even separated for a short while, but then we got back together. Julia promised me she would change, that she loved me. I decided to give us a second chance. But she couldn't change, not really. She started going out at night, drinking. Left me at home looking after Tyler, he would have been about eight or nine at the time. I didn't mind, he was a good kid. But Julia? She was drinking too much. Her moods were growing worse, really black and violent. One night she staggered in at two o'clock in the morning. I hadn't

173

heard her, I was in bed. I was fast asleep. Something woke me. I'm not sure what, I don't think it was Julia. A car outside maybe, or perhaps my subconscious had an idea what was going on and woke me up. Anyway, whatever the reason, I woke up and Julia was on the bed, straddling me. She was leaning over me, just staring at me. And she had a knife.'

Kirstin's hand flew to her mouth.

'Julia had this crazed look in her eyes. Even in the dark, I mean there was some light from the street outside but not much, but even so I could see this manic glare in her eyes. She was just about ready to lose it, and I knew that any move I made, even the smallest of movements, was going to send her over the edge. And I was probably going to wind up dead.'

'Oh no, you must have been terrified,' Kirstin said.

'Yeah.' Josh nodded. 'We stayed like that all night, her staring at me with that knife in her hand and me staring right back at her. It was just about when dawn was breaking that her eyes started closing and her head nodding with sleepiness, and I took my chance and grabbed that knife off of her.'

Naomi squeezed Kirstin's hand and held it tight.

'I'm so sorry,' Kirstin said.

'That wasn't the end of it though. That day, once she was sober, I tried talking to her, tried to find out what was going on. Turned out she'd been sleeping around again and spending all my money. I had a business servicing airplane engines and like a fool I had made Julia a partner. She took the money and spent it all. Every last penny. I guess you don't really know anyone until you've spent time with them, lived with them, and then it's too late. I'm never sharing my life with anyone again. It's safer being alone.'

Kirstin's heart and stomach seemed to shrivel up a little at those words. Both Kirstin and Josh had been betrayed and hurt. Kirstin had thought she would never be able to trust another man again, that she could never open up her heart like that. But now she realised that this was exactly what had been happening with Josh. Over the last couple of days a bond had begun to grow between them. At least, Kirstin knew now, in her heart these feelings had flourished. But not Josh.

They walked on in silence. Finally they arrived at a spot where they had to stop and rest. The gradual, rocky climb turned into a sheer rock face, beside which the river tumbled down in a roar of white water.

'I've got to rest!' Naomi yelled over the thunderous roar of the waterfall.

Josh pointed to their right, where the mountain side dropped into the forest below. 'I think there's a space down there where we can rest in a little more peace and quiet!'

Josh led the way down a narrow, precipitous path. Kirstin stepped carefully, running one hand along the rocks to steady herself. The sheer drop into the forest gave her vertigo. But Josh was right, and they found a shelf to rest on, overlooking the forest and away from the thundering power of the river plummeting down the rock face.

They all took long drinks from their water bottles. Kirstin wiped her forearm across her forehead. 'I am so sweaty,' she said. 'I could really do with a shower.'

'If that waterfall wasn't so powerful you could have stood under there,' Josh said.

'How much further do we need to go?' Naomi asked.

Kirstin pulled the map from her rucksack and unfolded it. 'It's difficult to tell using just this hand-drawn map, but I don't think we can be too far from where the cross is marked on the map.'

Josh and Naomi both leaned in close and stared at the grubby sheet of paper.

Josh smiled. 'X marks the spot, as they say.'

'If only X really did mark the spot,' Naomi said.

'Like in a computer game?' Kirstin asked.

Naomi tipped her head back and groaned. 'Wouldn't that be great? We could have breaks from playing and go back to the normal world.'

'That's right, and if you died you'd always have another life to try again,' Josh said.

'And we could set the game on easy mode,' Kirstin said.

They all thought about this for a few moments.

'What's that down there?' Naomi said.

Kirstin and Josh looked where she was pointing. A shape, tangled in the undergrowth on a rocky outcrop. A shape that looked to Kirstin like a body.

Josh stood up. 'I'm going down there for a closer look.'

'Are you sure?' Kirstin said.

'Don't worry, I'll be careful.'

Josh lowered himself over the edge of their resting place, holding onto roots and vines. Kirstin watched anxiously as he climbed down, taking his time to find decent hand and foot holds. In places he had to fight his way through the tangle of branches and leaves and thick vines. Finally he reached the outcrop where the body lay, and he bent over it, checking for signs of life.

Kirstin watched as Josh straightened up and looked up at her.

'It's Moses!' he called out. 'He's dead!'

14

'Do you think it was an accident?' Kirstin said.

They were standing by the waterfall again. It had seemed wrong to stay where they could see the body. Naomi had said they should bury him, but Josh had pointed out they would need to drag Moses' body somewhere they could dig a hole in the ground, and that was going to be practically impossible.

Nobody answered Kirstin's question. After all, that wasn't the real question she had been asking. And they all knew what that was.

Had Moses been murdered?

Since losing his finger to the piranhas, Moses had become a liability to Charles and Julia. He had only really been of use to them because of his knowledge of boats, and his supplies. But on land, and growing slowly sicker and weaker, he was just slowing them down. But were

Charles and Julia callous enough to simply kill him? Kirstin could believe it of the silent and menacing Oddball. But Charles? The man she had married?

Kirstin could see that Josh and Naomi were both struggling with the same thoughts. Perhaps there had always been the possibility of events taking a sinister turn such as this, but now that it had finally happened a line had been crossed.

They were in a new world now. One where the normal rules of life no longer applied.

'I don't think it was, no,' Josh said, finally. 'I think Charles and Julia decided to get rid of Moses as he was slowing them down too much.'

'But what about Oddball?' Naomi said. 'Couldn't he have done it?'

'To be honest, he was probably the one to throw Moses over the edge,' Josh replied. 'But he only did it because Charles and Julia ordered him to. He does nothing of his own willpower, only what he is ordered to do.'

Despite the heat, Kirstin shuddered.

'That poor man,' she said. 'I know he betrayed us, but no-one deserves that.'

'The thing is,' Josh continued, 'if Moses was slowing them down so much that Charles and Julia decided murder was a justified solution, they probably aren't that far ahead. Now the question is, do we really want to catch up with them?'

'You think we should head back?' Naomi said.

Josh's face was grim. 'I think we should seriously consider it.'

Kirstin still had the photocopied map clutched in her hand. She'd forgotten all about it, but now, talking about the journey once more, she remembered they had been looking at it. Unfolding the badly stained and creased sheet of paper once more, she stared at the crude map, willing it to give up its secrets.

'We're so close,' she said. 'I know we are.'

Josh leaned in close to Kirstin and looked at the map. 'If we're that close then Charles and Julia are already there.

They've found the Lost City, they beat us to it.'

Kirstin turned away. She knew Josh was right, she knew that everything he said made sense. They should turn around and head back. By tomorrow they could be back in civilisation, cleaned up and rested. The day after that they could be flying back to the UK, back home to family and friends. And safety.

This wasn't about Kirstin anymore. This was about Naomi and her future. Already Kirstin had placed her in danger too often, and yet Kirstin continued to make the same mistakes. But now, confronted with a murder, surely she had no choice but to make that decision to turn around and go home?

Kirstin looked at the map again. The Lost City of Quetzalcoatl. A dream she had been chasing almost her whole life, and now it had turned into a nightmare. And still it was out of her reach.

Yet so tantalisingly close.

Kirstin stared at the X on her map. 'It feels like . . . it feels like we're already here. That we're on top of it. That we're missing something.'

Josh placed a gentle hand on her shoulder.

Kirstin continued to stare at the X.

X marks the spot.

She lifted her eyes from the sheet of paper and looked at the water crashing against the rocks at the bottom of the waterfall.

X marks the spot.

Was it her imagination, or could she see an X in the water? Of course not, her exhausted mind was playing tricks on her.

Kirstin blinked and looked again.

It was still there. Fissures in the rock created the illusion of a giant X, just visible beneath the foam of the water crashing onto it.

'Hey, look at that,' she said, and pointed. 'X really does mark the spot.'

★ ★ ★

'This is crazy,' Josh said as a fine spray of water hit him in the face. He was starting to get seriously fed up with saying this and being so negative all the time. But he had no choice. It was crazy. They had climbed down a steep slope to get as close as they could to the river and the X. Now that they were up close and viewing it at a different angle, the X was no longer visible. But Kirstin knew it was still there.

X marks the spot.

The idea was ridiculous, but what if her grandfather really had meant that X literally marked the spot on his map? The only conclusion she could reach was that they were here. They had found the Lost City of Quetzalcoatl. But if that was the case, where on earth was it?

The day suddenly dimmed, as though a curtain had been pulled across the sun. Kirstin glanced up to see thick, dark clouds rolling in.

'Here's that storm coming in, just as I was afraid of,' Josh said, pointing to the mountain range in the distance.

The peaks of the mountains were no longer visible, now hidden by heavy, black clouds. A flash of forked lightning illuminated the gloomy horizon. Kirstin counted in her head. She reached six before she heard the distant rumble of thunder.

'We need to find shelter, and soon,' Josh said.

'Mum?' Naomi moved in closer to her mother. 'I think he's right.'

Kirstin slipped her arm around Naomi's shoulders. 'Of course he is. Let's find shelter and then head home, shall we?'

Naomi nodded. Kirstin glanced back at the waterfall, a part of her still desperate to stay, to puzzle this out. As she did so the sun broke through the cloud cover, the shaft of light shining on the curtain of water tumbling from above. The water sparkled in the light. And behind the wall of water, Kirstin saw a shadow.

'I've found it!' she shouted. Kirstin looked at Naomi and then at Josh. 'I've found it, I know where the Lost City is!'

15

The rain started falling. Huge, fat drops smacking into the ground. The clouds had closed in again and the last of the sunlight disappeared.

'We need to find shelter, now!' Josh said.

A brilliant flash of lightning threw the forest and the river into bright, harsh relief. In the gloom following the lightning burst, Kirstin could still see the ghostly image of the waterfall. The drops of rain turned into a deluge of water, drenching Kirstin, Naomi and Josh in a moment.

Kirstin pointed at the waterfall. 'The Lost City is through there!'

Josh shook his head. 'Forget about that, we need to get somewhere out of this rain.'

Kirstin stared at Josh. She could see that there was no way she was going to convince him. Perhaps he even thought

187

she had gone a little crazy right now. And maybe he was right. But Kirstin knew she had found the Lost City of Quetzalcoatl, and she wasn't going to let anybody stop her from exploring it.

Kirstin grabbed Naomi's hand. 'I love you.'

Naomi looked tearfully at her mum, rainwater streaming down her face. 'I love you too, Mum.'

'Do you trust me?'

Naomi nodded.

'Then come with me.'

Kirstin stepped into the rushing water. Her boot filled with water immediately. She put her other foot in the river. Naomi followed her.

'What are you doing?' Josh shouted.

'Finding shelter,' Kirstin said, looking back at Josh standing on the bank. 'Come with us or stay there, it's up to you.'

She hated doing this, but she knew it was the only way to get Josh to follow her. He was way past being swayed by persuasive arguments now. Kirstin just had to hope he would stick with them and not give up and leave them here alone.

Gripping Naomi's hand tight, Kirstin turned to face the wall of water just in front of them, thundering to the rocky ground beneath their feet. 'We're going to walk into the waterfall, alright?'

'Mum, I'm scared,' Naomi said.

'Don't be, it's all going to be alright.'

And with that, Kirstin walked into the deluge of falling water and took Naomi with her.

Kirstin had thought that the rain had battered them, it was so heavy and torrential. Turned out that was nothing compared to the gallons of water pounding them as it hurtled from a ledge high above. In the middle of the waterfall the breath was sucked from her lungs and she had to will herself to not try and breathe in. Naomi had bent at the waist as the water pounded on her back.

Keep moving, Kirstin thought. Keeping hold of Naomi's hand and pulling her closer, Kirstin took another step forward, and another.

Suddenly they were out of the falling water. They were standing on a rocky ledge. The curtain of falling water was behind them, and in front was a cave. Naomi threw her arms around Kirstin and held her tight.

Josh stepped through the wall of water. His mouth opened in astonishment.

'I see you found us some shelter,' he said.

The cave stretched back into darkness. A faint light managed to fight its way through the waterfall, but in the gloom that had fallen over them it was weak and pitiful. Kirstin could only imagine what it must look like when the sun was shining on the water and into the cave. She could picture bursts of sunlight sparkling over the rocky walls. Kirstin sat down on a rock and Naomi joined her. She wiped water off her face.

'I'm drenched through,' she said.

Josh lowered himself to the rocky ground and pulled his rucksack off his back. 'Me too, but at least we're not getting rained on anymore. Hey, well done for spotting this. It was a good call.'

Kirstin smiled. 'Thank you.'

'We can rest up here for the rest of the day and wait for the storm to pass. We'll get drenched again stepping back through the waterfall, but that can't be helped.'

'We're not going back,' Kirstin said.

'What are you talking about?' Josh said. 'Of course we're going back. Where else do you — ?'

'That way.' Kirstin pointed into the dark depths of the cave. 'That's the way to the Lost City, and that's where we are headed next.'

Josh looked like he was about to object, and Kirstin prepared herself for an argument. But then his shoulders sagged, and he shook his head, grinning.

'There's just no stopping you, is there?'

Kirstin grinned back. 'Nope.'

'Alright, I give in.' Josh looked into the darkness of the cave. 'But why you expect to find a city in the middle of a cave is beyond me.'

'Let's go find out, shall we?' Kirstin

said.

They gathered up their backpacks and hoisted them on to their shoulders. Kirstin had a lantern and when she switched it on it flooded the cave with light. Rocky protrusions cast shadows that came alive with every movement of the lantern. The cave extended into the mountain, but there was no clear path to walk along. If they were going that way, they were going to have to climb and scramble across the rocks.

And it wasn't going to be easy.

Kirstin took the lead, with Naomi behind her and Josh at the rear. They moved slowly, taking their time to climb carefully over the rocky ground. Kirstin was acutely aware that one misstep might well result in a broken ankle or worse. And then they would be in serious trouble.

What seemed like hours and hours passed slowly and they grew tired and hot. At least their clothes had dried, but Kirstin was starting to lose faith that they would find the Lost City of Quetzalcoatl after all. Josh was right, how could she expect to find a city in the middle of a cave? The cave would have to be huge, and then there was the matter of sunlight and rainfall.

An underground city just wasn't possible. It was something out of a science fiction book.

Maybe she should suggest they turn back. She had done her best to find the Lost City, but perhaps now was the time to give up her dream of ever finding it. Perhaps it didn't even exist, but was just a myth after all. Maybe her grandfather had never found it, even knew himself that it had been a myth, and his map was some sort of practical joke, or the result of a fever.

That had to be it. Walter had been so consumed with searching for the Lost City of Quetzalcoatl that he had fallen seriously ill, and when he recovered his mind tricked him into believing that he had found it. Could that really be what had happened? Had they all just been on a wild goose chase all this time?

Kirstin's heart grew heavy with this thought. It would be a sad way to end their journey into the heart of the Amazon rainforest.

'Hey!' Josh hissed from behind. 'Turn your light off.'

Kirstin stopped climbing over the rocks. 'Why?'

'Just do it.'

Kirstin turned off the lantern. Darkness swallowed them up. Except . . . was that a faint glow of light up ahead?

'What's that?' Naomi whispered. 'Is there somebody else in here with us?'

'I don't know,' Kirstin replied, keeping her voice low. Could it be Charles? Had they got here before them and found the cave?

Kirstin waited and watched. There was a definite possibility that Charles and the others could have heard them scrambling through the cave and already knew they were here. But Kirstin didn't want to take any chances. If they could keep their presence a secret, then they didn't have to worry about Oddball coming after them. Charles and Julia obviously had no scruples about getting rid of anybody who stood in their way anymore, even if it meant killing them. Kirstin shuddered.

'The light's not moving,' Josh whispered.

Maybe it wasn't Charles after all. In fact, now that she thought about it, Kirstin realised the light was more of a general glow, almost ethereal.

'Let's get closer, see what it is,' Kirstin said.

She didn't switch the lantern back on. Now that her eyes had grown accustomed to the faint light, she felt she could see well enough to make her way carefully over to the source of the glow. If she switched the lantern back on, it would only dazzle her. The three of them climbed slowly through the cave, drawing closer to the faint glow of light. Kirstin realised it was coming from behind a corner. She could see the outline of the rocks, shadows forming as the light grew stronger.

'That's not a torch,' Josh said.

'It looks kind of like daylight,' Naomi said.

Placing her hand against a large, smooth rock to steady herself, Kirstin pulled herself around the corner in the cave's passage.

A beam of soft light fell from the cave's ceiling, illuminating a cavern the size of a cathedral. Kirstin looked up. Long stalactites hung from the ceiling, moisture dripping from their tips and falling to the ground. But high above them, in the cavern's ceiling, was a hole and it was through this that sunlight was shining.

'Wow, that's amazing,' Naomi whispered.

'It looks like the storm has passed,' Josh commented. Kirstin climbed over to the beam of light and stepped underneath it. She looked up, but she couldn't see the top of the opening.

'Do you think we are near the surface?' she said. Josh and Naomi joined her.

'I'm not sure, but I get the feeling not,' Josh said. 'I would imagine we are pretty deep inside the mountain now. This looks like a sinkhole of some sort.'

'Could we get out that way if we needed to?' Kirstin said.

'I doubt it. It looks pretty inaccessible to me.'

Kirstin took a look around the cavern. A huge vertical split in the cavern wall gave them an exit. In fact, it looked a lot more accessible than the route they had been taking so far.

Naomi sat down on the cavern floor. 'I'm exhausted. Can we rest for a bit, please?'

'Of course,' Kirstin said. She pulled her rucksack off her back and sat down next to her daughter and placed her arm around her shoulders. 'You're doing brilliantly.'

Naomi smiled. 'Thanks, Mum.'

Josh groaned as he sat. 'Man, I am so tired.'

'At least we've dried off now,' Kirstin said. 'Although I desperately need a shower and a hair wash.'

Naomi took the rucksack and placed it

against a rock. She lay down and rested her head against it, using the backpack as a pillow.

'It's so peaceful here,' she said. 'It's like being in a church.'

Naomi was right, Kirstin realised. For the first time in weeks there was no surrounding noise. No birds screeching, no shuffle of creatures in the undergrowth, no noisy river or waterfalls. Apart from the occasional drip of water from a stalactite, there was silence.

Kirstin's eyes began to droop. So tired. Perhaps it would be a good idea to rest here for a while. Kirstin gazed at the cavern wall as sleep began to swallow her up. What was that on the rock face? She hadn't noticed it before. As her head drooped and sleep finally took her, a last thought formed and then slipped away before it could take hold. Was that a drawing of some sort on the cave wall?

16

The jagged edges of the hard, rocky ground dug into Kirstin's back. Her spine felt locked in place and her shoulders ached. How could she have fallen asleep in here? Reaching out a hand, she found Naomi asleep beside her. Kirstin thought she should open her eyes, but her eyelids were gummed together and despite the discomfort she didn't want to properly wake up just yet. Movement meant more pain.

'Kirstin, wake up.'

That was Josh, speaking softly as though he didn't want to disturb her. But if he didn't want to disturb her, why was he telling her to wake up?

'Kirstin, wake up.'

Kirstin groaned. He wasn't going to leave her alone. Why was that? Was there something wrong? Her chest filling with a sudden anxiousness, Kirstin dragged her gummy eyelids open. The cave was unnaturally bright and Kirstin had to squint. Even so, she could make out the silhouettes of the figures standing over her.

Kirstin struggled up to a sitting position. Her vision slowly cleared. Kirstin, Naomi and Josh were surrounded by a group of Amazonian warriors. Holding spears pointed at their captives, the villagers stared angrily at them.

A woman spoke, but in a language that Kirstin didn't understand, or even recognise.

'I think she's telling us to get on our feet,' Josh said.

'Do you understand her?' Kirstin whispered.

'No, but she's raising her hand, indicating we should rise. At least I think that's what she means.'

'You are correct, you must stand.'

A woman stepped forward between the warriors. She also looked like a warrior, strong and athletic. Her English was clear and distinct, without even the trace of an accent. Naomi took her mother's hand and shuffled in close to her.

'Can you help us, please?' Josh said. 'We have no bad intentions, we don't want to cause any trouble.'

'You must stand,' the woman repeated.

'Alright, we must stand,' Josh muttered.

He clambered stiffly to his feet and then helped Kirstin and Naomi up. The warriors, a mix of men and women, stepped back. They kept their spears trained on their captives.

The first warrior woman pointed at the vertical split in the cavern's wall and spoke again.

'You are to come with us,' the English speaking warrior said.

Josh looked at Kirstin. 'I don't think we have much choice.'

Two of the warriors led from the front and the rest followed behind Kirstin, Naomi and Josh. As they headed for the gap in the wall, Kirstin noticed the cave drawing that she had seen last night as she was falling asleep. A tingle of electricity shot through her body as she realised what it was. The legendary South American god, Quetzalcoatl.

They had to walk in single file through the crevasse, but the way was easier going that it had been previously. It almost seemed like a well-trodden path. They hadn't been walking too long before the rocky walls on either side of them opened out. They gathered together on a large rocky outcropping and looked out across the largest cavern Kirstin had ever seen. And she gasped in astonishment at the sight that met her.

Down below and stretching into the distance lay a dense forest, illuminated by shafts of soft sunlight. A network of rope bridges had been constructed between trees and houses built on stilts or in the trees themselves. A river snaked its way through the forest, appearing and disappearing between the densely packed trees. Kirstin saw birds landing in the treetops and then fluttering back out again.

In the distance, Kirstin saw a massive waterfall. That had to be the source of the river they had been following. She let her gaze wander up the waterfall's route to see if she could spot where it entered the massive cavern, but it disappeared into cloud cover. Kirstin grabbed Josh's arm as she suddenly felt a little giddy.

Cloud cover! This cavern was so big that, with the sunlight from the sinkholes in the roof, it had developed its own eco-system.

Kirstin had heard of a similar cave in Vietnam, but she had a feeling this one was even bigger.

A large, winged creature hurtled past. Its wings seemed impossibly long and Kirstin caught a glimpse of claws and a vicious beak. She ducked, and Naomi screamed.

Was it the winged god, Quetzalcoatl?

Kirstin straightened up as she realised the warriors were laughing and pointing at her.

'I can't believe it!' Josh said. 'Did you see that? It's a harpy eagle!'

Kirstin watched as the magnificent bird flapped its long wings and rose into the air. She felt more than a little foolish.

A gentle prod in the back from the end of a spear indicated to Kirstin that they needed to move again. The warriors led them down a steep set of steps carved into the rock face. Kirstin had to guide her hand along the rocky wall to steady herself. The steps were narrow and the drop down into the forest was a long one.

A group of children were waiting for them at the bottom of the steps, chattering excitedly and staring in wonder at the newcomers. They backed cautiously away at the sight of the newcomers, mouths open. Two of the warrior women shooed the children away. They ran, giggling, to the nearest tree where they climbed a rope ladder up to a bridge.

'Can you believe what you are seeing?' Kirstin whispered to Naomi and Josh. Naomi shook her head. 'I feel like I am in a fantasy film.'

The warrior women urged their captives on and they started walking again. They followed a path that undulated between trees and through rocky ground.

Kirstin glimpsed a lake with houses built on stilts along the shore. Were these caverns prone to flooding?

The path began ascending, growing steeper until it turned into steps once more. A rope had been installed to assist them and Kirstin grabbed it gratefully and hauled herself up the steps until they reached the top. Now they were on a new level, again densely packed with towering, thick trees. And up ahead, a wooden house built on stilts. Steps led up to a veranda where a young child sat and gazed with round eyes.

The warrior women prodded their captives, urging them on toward the dwelling. The child jumped to his feet and scampered inside, yelling.

An older woman stepped outside, the child by her side, his arms wrapped around her waist and his head resting on her hip.

'Who are you?' she called out. 'Why have you come here? How did you find us?'

Kirstin struggled to find an answer.

Her senses were overcome with the discovery of this new world underground.

Josh spoke. 'We're sorry, we don't mean to — '

The woman held out a hand and silenced him.

'You must remain quiet.' She pointed at Kirstin.

'You, talk, explain yourself.'

Kirstin blinked. Gathered her thoughts together.

'My name is Kirstin Ripley,' she said. 'This is my daughter, Naomi, and our friend Joshua Hanson. We don't mean any harm to you, we didn't even know you were here.'

A commotion from inside the house silenced Kirstin. A white man, dressed in the traditional dress of the villagers, stepped out and onto the veranda. He looked to be about the same age as the woman.

'Did you say your name is Ripley?' he said.

Kirstin nodded.

'And your father, what is his name?'

the old man said.

'John,' she replied.

The old man shook his head. 'No, no, I don't mean your father. What is his father's name, your grandfather, quick, what is his name?'

Kirstin hesitated, confused.

'Come on young woman, tell me, what is your paternal grandfather's name?'

'Walter,' Kirstin replied. 'Walter Ripley.'

The old man grabbed onto the edge of the veranda to steady himself. His eyes pierced into Kirstin's. 'Did he send you?'

Kirstin shook her head. 'No, he . . . he died a few months ago.'

The man nodded, as though this news didn't totally surprise him. 'You'd better come inside,' he said. 'I expect you have a few questions.'

* * *

The inside of the house was surprisingly comfortable. Before the old man explained himself, his guests were offered water and food in wooden cups and bowls. They accepted gratefully. All Kirstin needed now was a shower and a good sleep, and she thought she might start to feel human once more.

But her curiosity trumped the need for sleep.

Kirstin needed answers.

As if reading her mind, their host said, 'You already know who I am, don't you, Kirstin?'

Naomi looked at her mother, her face a picture of astonishment. Kirstin squeezed her hand.

'Yes, I think I do. You're my grandfather's brother, aren't you? Edwin Ripley.'

Edwin smiled, and his face suddenly transformed into friendliness. 'That I am.'

'But . . . you look so much younger than you should,' Kirstin said. 'You look like you are in your sixties, but shouldn't you be in your eighties, or even nineties?'

'I've lost track of birthdays here, so I have no idea how old I am.' He paused and thought for a moment. 'Let's see, I do believe I was only three years younger than Walter.'

'Then that makes you ninety-two, or thereabouts,' Kirstin said.

'Whatever it is you've got, I'd like some of it please,' Josh said. 'You look amazing.'

'I think the climate here agrees with me,' Edwin replied.

'But, I thought you died,' Kirstin said. 'We found your grave, and your skeleton!'

'As you can see, I am perfectly alive and healthy,' Edwin said, spreading his hands out. 'The skeleton you found was that of a travelling companion who joined Walter and I late in our expedition. He stumbled into the trap that had been laid there, no doubt to catch animals, not people, and was killed instantly.'

Kirstin shook her head, trying to break free of the fog of confusion she felt lost in. 'I don't understand. What happened to you? And why did Walter never speak of you?'

209

Edwin nodded slowly and thoughtfully. 'I know it must seem strange to you, but we had our reasons. When our friend died in the pit dug into the forest floor, I decided it was time to turn back. I no longer had any desire to live in the so called civilised west any longer.'

'And so you and Walter parted ways at that point?' Josh said.

Edwin nodded again. 'And we agreed Walter should say I had gone missing in the rainforest and that he would never talk of me again.'

Naomi spoke up for the first time. 'But why?'

Edwin looked at Naomi kindly. 'Because we wanted this place to remain lost. If my family and friends had known that I was still alive they might have come looking for me. And having westerners descend upon this place, bringing their modern ways of living and all the publicity would have been a disaster for this incredible people.'

'But we found a piece of tin, with a map cut into it,' Kirstin said.

'I begged Walter to destroy that. It was a tobacco tin that Walter hammered out flat and then cut the map into. We had made a promise to never reveal the location of this village, but Walter couldn't quite let go. He needed some way of finding his route back here if the lure of this place became too much for him.'

Kirstin took a deep breath. There was so much to think about.

'He never said anything,' she said. 'He never told us that he had found the Lost City of Quetzalcoatl.'

Edwin chuckled. 'That's because he didn't. This isn't the Lost City.'

'It isn't?'

'No, your grandfather never found it.'

Disappointment flooded Kirstin's chest.

'But I did,' Edwin said.

17

Before answering any more questions, Edwin told them to wash up and rest. He said there would be plenty of time for questions and answers. Kirstin didn't argue. She was absolutely dead on her feet. She couldn't remember ever feeling this tired before. And from the look of Naomi and Josh, they both felt the same too.

Kirstin hadn't known what to expect for washing facilities. If pressed, she might have imagined a bowl, flannel and some cold water from a stream.

As it turned out, the villagers had showers. Each one was a cubicle, the walls weaved out of thin branches and giving privacy yet allowing a luxurious sensation of freedom. The shower itself was operated on a rope pulley system and the water was pleasantly warm. Soap was a natural liquid soap that smelt vaguely of tea tree oil. They each took it in turn to shower, Naomi going first.

Edwin's wife provided them with clean clothes; simple garments, light and airy and clean. Finally, they were shown to their bedrooms. The beds were little more than mats laid on the floor, but they were surprisingly comfortable. Even so, Kirstin didn't believe she would be able to sleep as she had so many questions flying around in her brain. She fell asleep immediately.

When she awoke it was night and the house was alight with tiny, flickering flames. They were almost magical, like fireflies or tiny angels.

Kirstin sat up and stretched. She grimaced at the pains shooting across her shoulders, down her back and along her legs. Despite the fact that she ached in pretty much every part of her body, she felt rested and energised. She was ready to ask some questions now. And she needed answers.

'Hey, sleepy-head,' Josh said, grinning.

Josh and Naomi were already up and in the main living area with Edwin.

'Hey, yourself.' Kirstin sat by Naomi. 'How long have you two been up?'

'Not long.' Naomi cuddled in close to her mother. 'We didn't want to wake you.'

A gentle, cool breeze circulated through the rectangular openings in the walls. Outside she could see the growing light of a new morning.

'Do you get winds down here?' Kirstin said, looking at the leaves waving softly outside.

'Only gentle ones, sometimes,' Edwin said. 'The cave is a closed system with its own environment, but sometimes the outer world and its atmosphere makes its presence felt.'

'I have so many questions,' Kirstin said. 'I just don't know where to start.'

Edwin smiled. 'Why don't you start with the most pressing ones?'

'I suppose so.' Kirstin shifted position, getting herself comfortable. 'Why did you decide to stay here? You could have come back home, you . . . '

'Could have returned to my family?'

Edwin said. 'Been an uncle to your father? A brother to your grandfather?'

Kirstin nodded.

Edwin sighed. 'I lost much in life when I made the decision to return here and settle down. I wasn't even sure the villagers would allow my presence. After all, I couldn't speak their language, I had no knowledge of their traditions or culture. And I was a stranger, potentially a hostile stranger who could have brought immense harm to their way of life. Maybe even wiped it out completely.'

'Then why did they let you stay?' Josh said.

'Because of Iliana.' Edwin gestured to his wife, who came and sat down by him. 'We were in love, and she trusted me and I her. There were no barriers between us except the temporary one of language. And that could be overcome with time and patience.'

'Edwin and I had said our goodbyes,' Iliana said. 'I had watched him leave with Walter, knowing I would never see him again.' Iliana took Edwin's hand and smiled at him. 'But then he returned, he came back for me, and I knew he would never leave me again.'

'Iliana had to petition the elders to allow me to stay,' Edwin said, smiling back at his wife. 'To this day she refuses to tell me how she persuaded them, but persuade them she did.'

Iliana laughed and shook her head.

'See?' Edwin said. 'She says nothing.'

'But the Lost City of Quetzalcoatl,' Josh said, leaning forward. 'You told us last night that you found it.'

Edwin nodded. 'And Walter almost found it too, he was so close it broke my heart the day I saw it. But perhaps it was for the best. If Walter had seen the city, then perhaps he might have decided to stay here too.'

'But then he never would have met my grandmother and they wouldn't have had my father,' Kirstin said.

'But then you never would have existed!' Naomi cried out. 'Which means I wouldn't have, either.'

'Well, I for one am glad your grand-father and grandmother met,' Josh said, turning to Kirstin and giving her a lop-sided grin.

Kirstin stifled her own smile. What had Josh meant by that comment? Just yesterday he had been telling her about how he could never trust another woman again after his marriage to Julia. And now he was saying things like this?

Pushing the troubling, but pleasing, thoughts out of her head, Kirstin turned her attention back to the reason they were here in the first place.

'You said you found the Lost City?'

Edwin nodded. 'It is here, in this underground cave system. The City of Quetzalcoatl is where the villagers used to live, or rather the villagers' ancestors. It has been abandoned for many hun-dreds of years and is flooded regularly during the rainy season.'

Kirstin's heart thumped with excite-ment. She could hardly believe she had found the legendary Lost City, a place so hard to find that many explorers did not believe it existed. If only her granddad could have been here too.

'Can you take us to it?' Kirstin said.

Edwin smiled. 'Of course. We shall wait for the daylight to return and then I shall take you. It's not too far.'

Naomi squealed and squeezed her mum tight. 'You found it, Mum! You found it!'

'We found it,' Kirstin said, hugging Naomi back. She looked at Josh and gave him a smile.

He grinned. 'We sure did.'

★ ★ ★

The soft light of the new dawn slowly illuminated the village and one by one the candles were snuffed out. The village gradually came to life and children gathered at Edwin and Iliana's hut, eager to see the newcomers. They seemed particularly intrigued with Josh and approached him cautiously whenever his back was turned but retreated when he faced them. Josh soon caught on and turned it into a game. He stood with his back to them, pretending not to notice as the boys and girls crept closer. Finally he leapt around, pulling a ridiculous expression and roaring, and the children ran away, screaming and giggling.

Naomi sat with a small gathering of teenage girls and allowed them to stroke her white skin and long hair. Edwin had explained that he was the only white person the villager girls had encountered and so they were fascinated by the newcomers, particularly a girl of their own age.

Kirstin sat and watched as Naomi made friends with one village girl in particular. Even without a common language, the two managed to giggle together and communicate through gestures. Kirstin's heart filled with love and pride as she watched her daughter and her new friend wander off together into the heart of the village.

Kirstin and Josh took a stroll through the village while they waited for Edwin to get ready and take them to the Lost

City. They explored the upper veranda of the massive cave first. Kirstin could hardly believe the sights that met her. Below them was the lush, green forest with tree houses and bridges spanning the gaps between the huge tree trunks. Children ran between the trees and up and down the paths snaking through the forest. And through it all flowed the river.

The jungle was illuminated by shafts of soft light, like signs of the holy in a Hollywood film. Birds flew gracefully through the shafts of light sometimes, the sun catching the edges of their wings. Other birds called out from their hidden places in the forest, and Kirstin thought she heard deeper, more animal like calls too. Kirstin could see why many of the houses had been built high in the trees. During the rainy season that river would easily breech the sides and flood the village. Up here on the raised area there was less need for the houses to be raised from the ground.

Kirstin looked up, craning her head right back. Clouds. She could still hardly believe what she was seeing. Clouds floating in the sky of an enclosed eco-system beneath the earth.

'Have you got your head around what you're seeing yet?' Josh said. 'Because I sure haven't.'

'Isn't it amazing? I'm not sure I will ever be able to believe what I am seeing.'

They continued walking. As they walked, side by side, their hands brushed together. Kirstin felt like a bolt of electricity had shot through her body.

Josh made no mention of it, but then his hand brushed hers again. This time their fingers entwined briefly, let go, and then came together again. And then they were holding hands.

'Let's walk over to the waterfall,' Josh said, as though holding hands was the most natural, ordinary thing in the world.

Hand in hand they wandered over to the vertical waterfall thundering down the rock face. Fine spray splashed Kirstin's face, making her blink. They stood in companionable silence, watching the torrent of water.

She turned her face away from the spray and looked at Josh. 'Now tell me, Mr Hanson, what's going on?'

'Your guess is as good as mine,' he replied, turning to face Kirstin. 'But I'm kinda getting the feeling that I like you. A lot.'

'I'm kinda getting the same feeling about you,' Kirstin said.

Josh took a deep breath. 'You know, this isn't easy for me. But I'm guessing it's not easy for you, either. Both of us have been through some rough times, and neither of us are exactly trusting of the opposite sex right now, am I right?'

Kirstin nodded. She was too afraid to speak, too scared to interrupt Josh in case it broke the spell between them.

'The thing is . . . ' Josh took Kirstin's other hand in his. 'The thing is, I feel like I can trust you. I feel like there could be a chance for both of us to . . . I don't know, heal maybe. Together.'

'I feel the same way,' Kirstin said.

Josh smiled. 'Can we just take it slow and easy for a while though?'

'Of course,' Kirstin replied.

Josh's smile grew and then suddenly faded as he looked over Kirstin's shoulder and down the path they had just walked up. Kirstin turned to see what he was looking at. Naomi, sprinting up the path towards them, shouting something that Kirstin couldn't quite hear.

'Oh no,' Kirstin muttered. 'Something's wrong, something is terribly wrong.'

Naomi barrelled into Kirstin, wrapping her arms around her mother's midriff. 'It's Charles and Julia! They're here!'

Kirstin looked back down the path as a chill filled her chest. The tall, striking figure of Oddball sauntered up the path towards them, his long-legged stride covering the distance in no time.

'We are in big trouble now,' Josh muttered.

★ ★ ★

Charles looked like he had won first prize in a high school popularity contest. Something which surely, Kirstin reflected, could never have happened. But here he was, grinning from ear to ear, and strutting up and down outside Edwin's home as though he owned the place.

Which he probably thought he did.

Julia looked no less pleased with herself, standing beside Charles and holding a rifle casually by her side. Kirstin wasn't sure that Julia cared one way or the other about finding the Lost City of Quetzalcoatl, in fact Kirstin wasn't sure that even Julia knew what she wanted. Maybe it was simply coming out on top, beating everybody else to the prize, whatever that prize might be.

And Kirstin was convinced that victory for Julia was even sweeter knowing that it was Kirstin and Josh she had triumphed over. A crowd of villagers had gathered around them, keeping a respectful distance from Julia and her gun.

Oddball stood behind Kirstin, Josh and Naomi, urging them on with prods in their backs.

'Here they are!' Charles clapped his hands together like a little child who had just been told he was going to Disney-land after all. 'Isn't this amazing?' He opened his arms wide, taking in the village and the cave.

'It was a whole lot nicer before you turned up,' Kirstin said.

Charles threw back his head and laughed. It was all a little too theatrical for Kirstin.

'You are amusing,' Charles said, when he had stopped laughing. 'If you had been this amusing when we were together, I might have married you after all.'

'You've got this back to front,' Kirstin said. 'I dumped you, remember?'

'Yes, yes, whatever,' Charles said, turning away from Kirstin. 'Julia, bring Edwin out, would you dear?'

Julia's smile slipped. 'Do it yourself. What am I, your slave?'

The good humour faded from Charles' face too. 'My dear, what did you say?'

'You heard me. I'm sick of you ordering me around all the time.' Julia pointed at Oddball. 'Why don't you ask Lurch over there to do your dirty work for you?'

'Oddball is looking after Kirstin,' Charles replied.

'Then go get the old man yourself. I've had enough of being pushed around.'

Charles sighed, as though disappointed with a sullen child. 'Oddball, go and bring Edwin out here would you, there's a good man?'

The big man walked silently into the house. Kirstin wondered if he ever talked. Or perhaps he never could. And she wondered what hold Charles had over him that he obeyed every command without question.

Holding Edwin by the arm, Oddball dragged him outside. Kirstin cried out when she saw the bruising on his face.

'What did you do to him?'

'For an old man he's very feisty,' Charles said. 'Edwin was rather impolite when we first arrived, and Oddball had to teach him some manners.'

The realisation that Charles intended to kill them dawned upon her at that moment. Up until now she had questioned the idea, believing that Charles, as bad as he was, would not cross that line. Even after finding Moses, Kirstin had clung onto the faint hope that there had been an accident. Because surely Charles, the man she had once been married to, even if only for a few hours, would not commit murder?

She knew the truth now. Charles and Julia were cold-hearted murderers who would stop at nothing to get what they wanted. And they had gone too far to let Kirstin, Naomi and Josh live.

A cold fury gathered in Kirstin's chest. There was no fear, no despair, just simple anger.

'Edwin is going to take us to the Lost City of Quetzalcoatl,' Charles purred.

'And what then?' Josh said. 'Are you going to kill us all? Kill all the villagers too?'

'Oh, Mr Hanson!' Charles cried in a voice filled with mock outrage. 'What kind of person do you think I am? Of course not. Once we have explored the Lost City we shall leave them in peace. Of course, after I have published my findings their quiet little hamlet will grow in popularity and they may find they want to relocate.'

'You'll destroy them!' Josh shouted. 'This place will be crawling with snakes from big companies wanting to exploit it for everything they can, and they won't care who or what they have to destroy to get their own way.'

'I'm sorry, Edwin,' Kirstin said. 'We never should have come here. Granddad was right to try and keep this place a secret.'

Edwin said nothing, but Kirstin could see the blame in his eyes and she was ashamed.

'Enough,' Charles snarled. 'Let's get moving.'

Oddball dragged the old man down the steps from the veranda.

'Lead on,' Charles said.

Edwin pulled his arm free from Oddball's grip and began walking. Charles and Julia followed him. Oddball remained at the back, pushing Kirstin, Josh and Naomi on. And behind him followed the crowd of villagers.

What are we going to do? Kirstin thought. We just can't let Charles and Julia get away with this.

18

The procession halted. They had reached the river, the water rushing down a path carved in the rock, its power and fury frightening in its intensity. A simple rope bridge had been strung across the rapids. On the opposite bank, the trail disappeared into a dense, dark jungle.

'What are we waiting for?' Charles snarled. 'Over you go.'

Edwin gripped the rope handholds and stepped onto the basic bridge. Its base was a single rope with ropes attached either side along its length and stretching up to form a V shape with the handrails. Kirstin had a moment to wonder if the old man would be able to navigate the flimsy bridge, but he strode confidently across it to the other side.

'You next,' Charles said, pointing at Kirstin.

Taking a deep breath to try and calm herself, Kirstin put one foot on the thick rope. Gripping the ropes on either side, she stepped tentatively out over the bubbling, frothing water. The rope bridge swayed with every movement she made. Edwin had made this look so easy. She kept moving forward, fixing her eyes on the end of the rope, on the firm ground, waiting for her to step gratefully onto it.

The rope bridge swayed alarmingly with every movement she made. The sound of water pounding against the rocks filled her head. If she fell off this flimsy bridge, she would either be dashed against the boulders or swept off down the raging river. Or both probably.

In either case, she doubted she would survive.

'Keep looking at me!' Edwin shouted.

Kirstin snapped her head up and stared at the old man. She hadn't even been aware that she had paused and looked down at the raging river.

Keeping her eyes fixed on her grandfather's long-lost brother once more, Kirstin began moving again. All she had to do was put one foot directly in front of the other on the thick rope, whilst gripping the ropes at her sides.

Easy. Again the flimsy bridge swayed with every movement Kirstin made. But, inch by delicate inch, she crossed the chasm and stumbled thankfully onto firm ground.

'He's sending Naomi over next,' Edwin said.

And right behind her came Josh.

'That's too many, that rope bridge isn't made for more than one person at a time,' Edwin said.

Kirstin sucked in a sharp breath of dismay as she saw the towering Oddball step onto the bridge directly behind Josh.

'What are they doing?' Edwin said. 'They'll get themselves killed.'

'It's Charles, he doesn't trust anyone,' Kirstin said. 'He's the one making them cross together.'

The rope bridge swayed wildly with three people crossing at the same time. Naomi had to stop and hang on as she was thrown from side to side. Right behind her, Josh looked ready to grab

Naomi if she fell.

Oddball pushed Josh in the back. Josh leaned down over Naomi's shoulder and said something in her ear. She nodded and began moving forward again. She looked close to tears.

'Keep your eyes on me!' Kirstin shouted. 'You're doing great!'

Josh followed right behind Naomi. And Oddball followed Josh, keeping very close to him. With the combined weight of the three bodies, the single length of rope bowed in the middle. A sudden thought chilled Kirstin to her bones. Oddball had already tried pushing Josh into a piranha infested river. What if he now attempted to throw him off the rope bridge? Josh would smash into the rocks below and almost certainly die.

Edwin gripped Kirstin's arm. 'There are too many of them, they're too close together, they need to spread out.'

Kirstin shook her head. 'Oddball's not going to let that happen.'

The procession kept moving, Naomi at the front taking it slow and steady.

Finally Naomi made it to the side and Kirstin pulled her close and hugged her tight. Josh stepped onto solid ground, closely followed by Oddball.

Kirstin let go of Naomi and shoved Oddball in the chest. 'You could have killed them out there!'

Oddball stared mutely down at Kirstin, his hooded eyes dark and unemotional. Josh grabbed Kirstin and pulled her away. 'Don't make him angry, we don't know what he will do.'

'Yeah?' Kirstin yelled. 'Well he doesn't know what I can do when I'm angry.'

Oddball just stared at her.

'Your friends are making their way over now,' Edwin said.

Kirstin stepped away from Oddball and watched Charles and Julia stepping carefully along the rope bridge.

'They're not our friends,' she said.

Kirstin turned her back on the swaying rope bridge, horrified at the thought that had slithered into her mind.

I wish they would fall and die!

No. Kirstin wouldn't allow herself to

start thinking like that. She would not lower herself to their level.

Finally, Charles and Julia climbed off the precarious rope bridge and onto solid ground. Kirstin refused to look at them.

'Lead on, old man!' Charles shouted in an exaggerated, cheery voice. 'We haven't got time to waste, you know.'

Edwin gave Charles a look of withering hatred, but then turned and did as he was told.

Following the old man in single file, they entered the dark, forbidding jungle.

★   ★   ★

Edwin had not brought torches. He must have known how dim and gloomy the forest would be. Had he forgotten in the stress of the situation, or had he not brought lights on purpose in an attempt to thwart Charles? But if that had been his reason, it hadn't worked. Charles, Julia and Oddball had torches and pulled them from their backpacks as the darkness of the forest swallowed them up.

They followed a path, snaking between the trees. Life stirred in the depths of the jungle; the rustle of undergrowth, the snap of a twig, the flapping of wings. It seemed to Kirstin that they were surrounded by creatures both small and large. But they stayed hidden, perhaps warily watching these intruders into their natural habitat. Kirstin hoped that was all they would do; watch.

A cry of pain brought them to a halt. Julia had stumbled and fallen to her knees. Kirstin watched as Charles helped Julia to her feet, the beams of light from their torches like searchlights in the night.

'Your knee is bleeding,' Charles said, bending down and examining it.

Julia shoved him away. 'Why on earth did you bring me here, you stupid man?'

'Julia, I —'

'Shut up!' Julia screamed. 'I hate you! And I hate this stupid place and these stupid people! I hate it all!'

Kirstin did her best to hide her smile, but it just seemed to keep growing and growing. She just hoped that in the gloom of the forest, Julia wouldn't be able to see it.

Charles turned on Edwin. 'You know this place, you knew how dark it would be in this godforsaken jungle! Why didn't you bring torches too?'

Edwin shrugged. 'Nobody asked me.'

Charles raised a hand as if to strike Edwin.

Josh stepped between them and grabbed Charles' wrist. Oddball, moving faster than Kirstin could imagine, picked Josh up like he was a child. Josh struggled and kicked, and Oddball threw him to the ground.

'Stop it!' Naomi screamed. 'You are all acting like spoilt children!'

A creature cried out in the depths of the jungle and another answered it. A sudden flapping of many wings in the foliage made them all jump.

Josh sat up, brushing dirt off his shoulders and back.

Oddball towered over him, looking ready to pick Josh up and throw him to the ground again.

'Charles, call your guard dog off,' Josh said.

'Oddball, leave him,' Charles said in a bored drawl.

Oddball stood over Josh for another second, staring down at him. Kirstin didn't think he was going to do as Charles had commanded him. The big man seemed to genuinely hate Josh. And if that was true, there might come a point where Oddball decided he wasn't going to listen to Charles anymore, at least where Josh was concerned.

Finally, Oddball stepped back.

Josh climbed gingerly to his feet, keeping his eyes on the towering henchman at all times.

'Is there some light over there?' Kirstin said, pointing to a soft glow just visible between the trees.

'Yes,' Edwin replied. 'There's a sinkhole, letting in light. We can rest there, it's only a couple of minutes' walk away.'

'No,' Charles snapped. 'No resting. Not until we reach the Lost City of Quetzalcoatl.'

They began walking once more. Edwin led the way and Kirstin followed right behind him with Naomi. Again she smiled as she heard Julia, all the way at the back, complaining of the pain in her knee. She was so dramatic.

The soft glow of light grew in brightness. The way the diffuse light broke into fragments as it filtered through the gaps in the branches and the leaves was beautiful and magical. The light almost seemed like a living thing.

Under other circumstances, Kirstin would have loved to have spent time here, savouring the natural beauty. But right now all she wanted was to escape and get back home to England. She wasn't sure she ever wanted to hear of the Lost City of Quetzalcoatl ever again.

If only Josh lived in England, too. Kirstin wasn't sure yet how deep her feelings ran for him, but she knew she wanted to find out. But how could they do that if they were living over a thousand miles apart?

Not forgetting that they had to escape

from this nightmare with their lives first.

They entered a clearing full of warm, soft light. A massive rock stood upright in the middle of the clearing, taller even than Oddball. It reminded Kirstin of one of the Stonehenge slabs. A giant, plumed bird had been carved into the dark stone.

Quetzalcoatl.

Edwin sat down on a flat rock, of which there were many set in a circle around the central block of stone. To Kirstin, it felt like a place of worship.

Charles prowled around the upright stone slab, examining the carving. For the moment he had forgotten everyone and everything else. The carving was decorated with gold edging, and what looked like it might be a precious stone had been used as the bird's-eye. Oddball bent down and gripped Edwin by his upper arm, hauling the old man to his feet. Josh stepped up close.

'Leave him alone,' he said, staring up into the giant's face.

Oddball's lips peeled back in what

Kirstin supposed was the strange man's attempt at a smile, or maybe a snarl. His teeth were rotten and black and jutted out at awkward, painful angles.

'Please, you're hurting me!' Edwin gasped.

'Let go of him now!' Josh snarled.

Their faces were only inches apart. Kirstin held her breath, waiting for someone to break the stalemate, waiting for the fighting to begin.

'Charles, please tell your manservant to back off,' she said.

Charles glanced absentmindedly at Oddball, and said, 'Put the old man down, we'll take a moment to rest here.'

Oddball released Edwin's arm, and the old man sat back down on the stone slab with a sigh.

Josh backed up, not breaking eye contact with Oddball who was still staring at him.

'Try not to antagonise him,' Kirstin whispered, when Josh had joined her and Naomi.

'And let him walk all over us?' Josh

said. 'Did you see how he was hurting Edwin?'

'I know,' Kirstin said, placing a gentle hand on Josh's arm. 'But look at him, look at how much he hates you. He just looks like he is waiting for the right moment to kill you.'

'Yeah, you're probably right,' Josh whispered. 'But I'm not going to give him the opportunity.'

'What are we going to do?' Kirstin said.

Josh rubbed his chin. 'I don't know, but we'll think of something. We have to.'

'I've got an idea,' Naomi whispered.

Kirstin glanced at the others. Charles and Julia had their backs turned, examining the carving on the massive slab of stone. Oddball also had his back to them as he stared at Edwin.

'What?' Kirstin whispered.

Naomi pulled a small bag with a drawstring from a pocket. 'Minika, the girl I made friends with, she gave me this.' Naomi opened the bag. Inside was a catapult and three hard-edged, sharp

242

looking stones.

Josh looked in the bag and then at Naomi. 'Can you even fire that thing?'

'Minika was teaching me before Charles turned up.'

Josh shook his head. 'A catapult's no good against them, especially Oddball. This isn't David and Goliath.'

'But I could distract them, and you could grab their guns,' Naomi whispered.

Josh shook his head again. 'No, it's too risky. Put that away again before the others see it.'

'What are you three whispering about?' Julia snapped. 'Charles! They're plotting something, I know they are!'

Charles approached them, an insolent smile playing over his lips. Josh stepped in front of Naomi, as though protecting her. Kirstin knew he was really giving Naomi a chance to hide the catapult in her pocket once more.

'Are you plotting something, Mr Hanson?' Charles said, his voice low and menacing.

'Of course we are,' Josh snapped. 'Do

you seriously think we want to stay here with you?'

Charles laughed. 'Your honesty is refreshing, at least. Let's get moving again, shall we?'

'But you said we could rest!' Naomi yelled. 'That poor old man is dead on his feet and you're going to kill him if you make him keep walking!'

'The three of you should have thought of that before you began whispering and gossiping with each other. Your mother and her boyfriend should at least have had more sense.'

Kirstin opened her mouth to protest, to tell Charles and everybody else that Josh wasn't her boyfriend. Instead, she closed her mouth without saying a thing. What was the point of rising to his bait? And besides, if she protested too much, Josh might get the wrong idea and she would lose him.

'Those two make a good pair,' Julia said. 'They're both as soft and feeble as each other.'

'You shut up!' Naomi yelled. 'You

don't know what love means. You don't even know how to be a decent human being.'

'Ooh, the little brat is having a tantrum, how sweet.'

Kirstin placed a hand on Naomi's shoulder. 'Ignore her, she's just taunting you.'

Edwin climbed slowly to his feet. 'I'm rested, let's go shall we?'

Edwin didn't look at all rested to Kirstin, in fact he looked exhausted. His eyes flicked over to Naomi and Julia and then back to Kirstin. And Kirstin realised he was doing this for Naomi, getting them moving again so that Julia would stop taunting Naomi.

Kirstin took a deep breath, quelling the urge to embrace Edwin and whisper a thank you in his ear. There would be time for gratitude later. Right now they needed to concentrate on not antagonising their captors.

Edwin took the lead once more, followed by Naomi and then Kirstin. Oddball, as usual, stuck doggedly to

Josh. Charles and Julia brought up the rear.

Kirstin was sad to leave the softly lit clearing with its stone slab and its carving. With the light there had seemed hope. At least a little. But now back in the gloom of the dense jungle, all sense of hope left Kirstin. All she had left to cling onto was a grim determination that she would not let Charles and Julia get away with this.

They had to pay for their crimes.

With Edwin at the front, progress was slow. It was increasingly obvious that despite his amazing good health, Edwin was feeling all of his ninety plus years. His confident stride had turned into a shuffle and he had begun stumbling more often.

How much longer could he keep going like this?

And what would Charles and Julia do if Edwin decided he could go no further?

Something else that worried Kristin were the noises from within the depths of the jungle. It was obvious to Kirstin that they were not on their own in here. She had seen no other signs of life, but she had heard plenty. The rustling of creatures creeping through the undergrowth and the flapping of wings above them.

But there was something more worrying her. It seemed to Kirstin that they were being followed. That some creature was keeping pace with them, running parallel to them but staying hidden in the dense thicket of trees.

A creature that may well have teeth and claws.

Edwin stopped walking.

'I'm so sorry,' he said to Kirstin as he slowly lowered himself to the ground.

Kirstin squatted down beside him. 'It's not your fault. It's mine, we never should have come here.'

Edwin was pale and sweaty. His hands trembled.

'What's the holdup?' Charles shouted from the back of the line.

'It's Edwin, he can't go any further,' Kirstin said.

Charles pushed his way past the rest of

the group. 'But he must, we can't afford to waste any more time.'

Kirstin looked up at Charles standing over them. 'He's an old man, look at him. You can't make him go any further, you'll kill him.'

Charles leaned forward, resting his hands on his knees. 'Where is it, you old fool? Where is the Lost City?'

Edwin raised a trembling hand and pointed down the gloomy, twisting path. 'Keep following the path. It's not far now.'

'How far?'

Edwin lowered his hand. 'Another ten minutes. Not far at all.'

Charles straightened up. 'Alright, we'll leave the doddery old fool here and carry on. We can collect him on our way back.'

Kirstin shook her head. 'No, we can't leave him here on his own. Charles, something has been tracking us, an animal. Haven't you heard it?'

'Nonsense,' Charles snapped. 'It's your imagination. We leave the old man here or we bring him with us now. It's up to you.'

Josh joined them. 'I'll stay and look after him.'

'No, you won't,' Charles snapped. 'You will come with us and do exactly as I tell you.'

'I will be fine,' Edwin said. 'Please don't worry about me.'

'At least leave him a torch,' Kirstin said.

'No,' Charles replied. 'The old fool knew how dark it would be in here, he should have brought his own torch.'

Kirstin and Josh swapped looks but said nothing. Leaving the old man here on his own was a bad idea, but there was nothing they could do about it. Charles was in charge.

Reluctantly, Kirstin left Edwin behind as they set off again. Now Charles led the way, and to Kirstin's horror he began whistling a cheerful little tune as he walked.

After another five minutes of stumbling through the gloom of the jungle,

Kirstin thought she could see another soft glow of light up ahead, leaking between the trees in faint beams.

And was that the river she could hear again?

They kept walking. Charles had begun to pick up his speed as the light grew stronger. Kirstin could feel the excitement radiating off him and, despite the situation, she felt the same way.

The Lost City of Quetzalcoatl!

She could hardly believe they were about to reach it.

The path was climbing now and Charles was huffing and obviously struggling. But still he kept going, walking faster and faster. The back of his shirt was soaked with sweat, and Kirstin could feel her own shirt sticking to her. The jungle thinned out. The daylight grew stronger.

Charles stopped abruptly and Kirstin almost collided into him.

She stepped up beside him as they were joined by the rest of the group. Kirstin felt Naomi's hand slip into hers, but she was hardly aware of it.

Her attention was consumed by the sight that met her eager eyes.

The Lost City of Quetzalcoatl.

19

Kirstin blinked, trying to make sense of the sight that met her eyes. Beside her, Charles seemed to be having trouble breathing. Kirstin could hear him panting, and then a tiny mewling noise began building in the back of his throat.

Glancing at him, she realised he was simply overcome with excitement.

She felt the same way.

The City of Quetzalcoatl was laid out in a grid pattern, reminiscent of New York City. But there the similarity ended. Instead of modern skyscrapers, there were ancient temples rising high above the streets. Many of the temples were topped with domed roofs, still glittering with patches of gold decoration that had not yet been worn away by the ravages of time. Others were more seriously damaged, with holes in their roofs and cracked sides. Some had collapsed entirely and lay in mounds of rubble on the ground.

Kirstin could see dwelling places and what once might have been gardens, but were now overgrown. From their vantage point up high, she thought she could also see a large courtyard, a gathering place perhaps, for a market.

And dotted everywhere, seemingly at random points, there were large stone slabs with drawings of Quetzalcoatl carved into them, the precious stones in their eyes sparkling in the light.

'It's . . . beautiful,' Charles whispered.

Josh and Naomi both joined Kirstin. She slipped her hands in theirs as they gazed out over the remains of the city.

'You did it, Mum,' Naomi said. 'You found the Lost City of Quetzalcoatl.'

Kirstin squeezed her hand. 'We did it. I never would have made it without you and Josh by my side.'

'We have to get down there,' Charles said, turning to Julia. 'We have to explore.'

'Oh, Charles, can't we just stop for a rest?' Julia flopped on the ground right where she was and sighed. 'My feet are killing me.'

Kirstin could hardly believe what she was seeing. Here they were at one of the greatest discoveries ever, and Julia just looked . . . bored.

Charles hardly noticed. 'We need to go down there right away.'

'Aren't you listening to me?' Julia screeched. 'I told you, I need to have a rest!'

Charles turned, finally distracted from the view. Kirstin flinched at the expression of hatred and venom on his face.

'Rest all you want, my dear!' he hissed. 'In fact, why don't you turn around and go back? I've had enough of your complaining, anyway.'

Julia, obviously finding hidden reserves of energy, scrambled to her feet and stuck her face in front of Charles'.

'How dare you! After everything I have done for you, you insult me?'

'And what, exactly, have you done for me? Been a thorn in my side, a dead weight around my neck, a constant annoyance in my ears . . . '

Julia slapped him across the face.

Oddball stepped forward, but Charles held out a hand to stop him. He rubbed at his red cheek.

'You will pay for that,' he said, his voice low and menacing.

'I already have,' Julia snarled, the contempt in her voice plain to hear.

Kirstin stood frozen still, waiting to see what Charles would say or do next. Josh and Naomi stood on either side of her, similarly transfixed.

Finally Charles turned away and looked down at the City of Quetzalcoatl once more.

'Let's go,' he said.

They naturally fell into step once more, Charles at the front and Oddball at the back. Julia kept her distance from Charles, but never took her eyes off him. They found a path leading down, and the path soon turned into a series of steps carved into the rock. The steps zigzagged back and forth down the steep rock face.

And below them, the City of Quetzalcoatl drew closer with every step they took.

Finally they reached the bottom. Kirstin breathed a sigh of relief. She had felt like an ant crawling down a wall, and one misstep would have sent her plummeting to her death.

Down amongst the remains of the ancient city the air felt moist and smelt of rotting vegetation. The streets and thoroughfares were overcome with tangled creeping vines and roots had erupted through the ground. Down here the sounds of birds chirruping and squawking was so loud it was almost uncomfortable, and underneath that Kirstin could hear the rustle of leaves and branches as creatures prowled through the forest.

The group wandered through the streets, picking their way carefully through the ruins.

An animal roar cut through the chatter of birds and other creatures and the group froze.

'I don't like the sound of that,' Josh muttered.

Kirstin looked around at the walls of

greenery strangling the ruins. 'It's that thing that has been tracking us, it's followed us down here.'

'Don't be ridiculous,' Charles snapped. 'We would have seen it on the steps.'

'Maybe there is another way down,' Josh said.

Charles turned his back on Josh and Kirstin in a gesture of utter contempt. 'We carry on.'

There was going to be no reasoning with Charles now as he had his eyes set on the prize. Up ahead, looming over the ancient ruins, stood a grand temple. Massive pillars rose into the sky, holding up a domed roof of gold and silver. Behind the pillars, a broad, stone stairway led inside the temple.

The group continued its approach, clambering over thick, gnarled roots and vines dripping with moisture. Even Julia had fallen silent.

When they reached the temple, they halted at the base of the steps. No-one had spoken, no-one had said they should stop. It just seemed the right thing to do.

Kirstin gazed in awe at the broad, stone steps, cracked and pitted with age. The temple had been built against the cave wall, and now Kirstin could see that the broad stairway led into the rock wall.

Into darkness.

Charles pulled a torch out of his backpack. 'Get your torches out, all of you!'

Kirstin and Josh looked at each other. They hadn't been given the option of bringing anything with them. They had no torches.

Julia and Oddball both pulled torches from their rucksacks. Charles began climbing the steps with Julia and Oddball behind him. Kirstin, Josh and Naomi stayed where they were.

Pausing, Charles turned and glared at them. 'What are you waiting for?'

'We don't have any torches,' Kirstin said. 'And we don't know what's inside, or how big it is. If we get lost, we might never find our way out again.'

A slow, unpleasant smile crept across Charles' features. 'Then you will have to stay close with us, won't you?'

'You could just let us go now,' Josh said. 'You've got what you wanted, you've found the Lost City, why do you even need us around anymore?'

'Perhaps I enjoy your company,' Charles sneered. 'Now, I'm not going to tell you again, get up these steps!'

Kirstin took Naomi's hand. 'Come on, there's no sense in aggravating him.'

They walked up the steps together and joined the others. Charles, Julia and Oddball shone the torches into the gloom of the temple's interior.

Kirstin took a deep breath.

And they walked into the temple.

★ ★ ★

At first the torchlight barely penetrated the darkness. They could see the ground they walked upon, the broken slabs of stone waiting to trip them, but they couldn't make out the sides of the temple. Or the ceiling.

'This place must be huge,' Josh whispered, and his words echoed eerily in the dark.

'Woohoo!' Charles called out and giggled as his voice bounced around the cave.

He's gone crazy, Kirstin thought. This expedition out here, finding the Lost City, it's all finally sent him over the edge.

They walked deeper into the darkness. Kirstin, Naomi and Josh held hands and kept close to the others with their torches. Kirstin glanced behind at the retreating rectangle of light that marked their exit. How far underground did this temple go?

Charles stopped walking and his torch light revealed a set of wide, uneven stone steps descending into more darkness.

'Down we go,' he said.

'This is utter madness!' Josh yelled, his voice bouncing off the walls. 'We don't know what's down there or even if we will be able to find our way out again.'

Julia let loose a high-pitched scream. Everyone flinched as the scream echoed around the temple.

Kirstin whipped around, expecting

to see whatever had been stalking them finally revealing itself. She imagined a giant lion or bear, eyes glowing with evil hunger and its jaws dripping hot saliva.

'Can't we just let them go?' Julia shrieked. 'I'm so sick of their pathetic arguing and whining.'

Kirstin relaxed as the fear drained from her body. There was no monster about to devour them, Julia was simply having a tantrum.

Charles thought for a moment. 'Perhaps you're right. Kirstin has served her usefulness after all.'

Hope blossomed in Kirstin's chest. Maybe they would make it out of here alive after all.

Charles produced a handgun from inside his jacket. 'But I can't let you go.'

Josh grabbed Naomi and pulled her behind him, shielding her from danger. And in that moment, despite the danger they were in, Kirstin knew that she was in love with this man. That she wanted to spend the rest of her life with him.

But first they had to escape from this

madman.

She drew in a shaky breath, and said, 'Charles, please, put the gun away.'

'I'm afraid I can't do that,' Charles simpered. 'You know too much, I can't risk you telling everyone about our little trip out here, can I?'

'So you're going to kill us? Silence us forever? The truth will still come out Charles, you know it will.'

'And just how will that happen, exactly?' Charles said. 'With you three silenced forever, I am free to tell whatever version of events I want to.'

A quick glance to the side showed that Oddball was pointing a gun at them too. Kirstin had thought of rushing Charles, gambling with the thought that he might be reluctant to shoot Kirstin despite what he said. But with Oddball pointing a weapon at her too, she knew she had no chance.

'Oh, just get on and shoot them, why don't you?' Julia wailed. 'I'm so bored with all this talking.'

Charles raised the gun.

A low growl echoed through the cave.

Despite her reluctance to tear her eyes off the gun pointed right at her, Kirstin glanced over her shoulder. Framed in the rectangle of light from the temple's entrance stood the silhouette of a big cat. That's what has been stalking us, Kirstin thought.

The animal sprang into movement, bounding towards them silently.

Charles and Oddball both fired their guns at the approaching creature. The sharp retorts echoed around the massive cave, but the bullets missed the big cat.

And then it was on them. The lithe creature reared up on its hind legs and dragged Charles to the rocky ground, snarling and growling. Charles screamed as he flung his arms up to protect himself and dropped the gun and his torch.

The torch rolled across the ground, close enough that Naomi was able to pick it up. Oddball levelled his gun at the writhing bodies on the ground, but he didn't shoot. In the wavering light of Naomi's torch, Kirstin saw that the big cat was a jaguar.

Charles screamed again as the jaguar roared, and then he fell silent.

Kirstin grabbed the torch from Naomi and turned the light away from the grisly scene.

'Quickly, let's get out of here,' Josh said, grabbing Naomi by her shoulders and turning her away from the awful spectacle.

Kirstin took her by the hand, but before they could make their escape the jaguar leaped in front of them and growled, baring its teeth at them.

Oddball pointed his gun at the big cat.

'Shoot it!' Julia yelled. 'Shoot it!'

Oddball did nothing, just kept the gun trained on the jaguar.

'He's waiting for it to attack us,' Kirstin whispered.

The jaguar's eyes shone in the light of the torch as it stared at Kirstin.

'Back up, slowly,' Josh whispered.

They all took a hesitant step back, Kirstin and Josh both flanking Naomi, protecting her as best they could. The big cat began prowling back and forth, never taking its eyes off Kirstin.

'What are you waiting for? Shoot it!' Julia hissed.

The jaguar shifted its attention to Julia.

Oddball pulled the trigger.

The gun made an empty click.

The big cat leapt at Oddball as Julia's piercing scream echoed around the massive cavern.

'Run!' Josh hissed.

They couldn't risk running past the jaguar and towards the exit of the temple cave, and so they turned and stumbled down the rocky steps leading into the depths of the cavern. In Kirstin's hand the torch wobbled and jumped, casting crazy shadows over the walls.

At the bottom of the broad flight of uneven steps they halted in front of two massive wooden doors. Kirstin played her torchlight over the doors to reveal carvings of winged creatures with claws. In the cave at the top of the steps they could still hear the jaguar growling, and

Julia screaming.

Josh planted his hands against the double doors and pushed. They gave slightly.

'Help me,' he said.

Kirstin and Naomi pushed at the huge doors with Josh. Grating raggedly against the ground, the doors began to open.

Kirstin stumbled through the widening gap first. Panting with the effort of pushing against the huge wooden door, she stumbled and then lifted her torch, the light illuminating her surroundings.

She screamed.

20

Quetzalcoatl was real. The legendary Aztec winged reptile was no myth after all, but a living, breathing creature. And here, deep in an underground temple in the heart of the Amazon and illuminated by the light of Kirstin's torch, was the proof.

Angular, winged creatures with vicious beaks and talons and glittering eyes crouched in the torchlight, staring balefully at the intruders. Kirstin trembled so hard she couldn't keep the torch steady and the light bounced from one creature to another.

There were so many of them, packed into this underground chamber. Their golden hued wings twitched and jerked to life as the creatures became aware of the three humans in their presence.

Kirstin's mind screamed at her to run, but her body refused to move. They had no chance. Before they had even turned back to the doors, they would be over-come by the giant reptilian birds.

Kirstin screamed again as she felt the first creature take her by the shoulder.

'Kirstin, it's alright, they're statues!' Josh hissed.

He snatched the torch from her hand and shone the beam of light steadily on the nearest creature.

'Statues?' Kirstin said, suddenly over-come with weakness. 'But I saw them move, I saw their eyes shining.'

'Their wings are decorated with gold, look.' Josh played the torchlight over the nearest creature's splayed wings. 'And their eyes are gems of some sort.'

Josh was right. As he shone the torch-light around the cavern and over the huddled bird-like monstrosities, Kirstin started laughing.

'Mum? Are you okay?' Naomi said.

Tears streamed down Kirstin's cheeks. She grabbed Naomi's hand.

'Hold on to me before I fall down,' she gasped.

After everything they had been through and she had come to this, thinking they were about to be killed by a bunch of statues.

'Let's see if there is another way out, before that jaguar decides to join us down here,' Josh said.

Hand in hand, the three of them threaded their way between the giant statues. Up close, Kirstin could see how beautiful they were. The gold decoration on their wings resembled feathers, and their talons were painted in vivid red.

But it was the eyes that still sent a shiver of fear through Kirstin. As they glittered in the torchlight, it seemed that they followed the three intruders through the cave, watching their every move.

Was this the rumoured treasure that lay waiting to be discovered in the Lost City of Quetzalcoatl? If so, Kirstin was happy for it to stay here. She shuddered at the thought of the rituals that might have been performed down here in ancient times, under the watchful eyes of these lizard gods.

'Do you really think this leads anywhere?' Naomi said, breaking into Kirstin's thoughts.

'I don't know,' Josh muttered. 'But I don't fancy that big cat's chances against Oddball, and I don't want to hang around and wait to find out which one wins their fight.'

'What about Julia?' Kirstin said.

'What about her?' Josh replied. 'If Oddball manages to kill that big cat then she's fine. If not, well, she made her own choices in life, and she's got to live with the consequences.'

Kirstin glanced at Josh, but it was hard to read his expression in the darkness. Did he really feel that way? After all, they had been married once.

'I can hear something!' Naomi whispered.

The three of them stood still and listened. Kirstin heard it too, a low rumble from deep within the cave.

'What is it?' she said.

Josh shook his head. 'I'm not sure. But we're headed for it, whatever it is.'

They began walking again, between more of the giant statues. As they walked, the rumble slowly grew louder.

'It sounds like a waterfall,' Kirstin said.

And even as the words left her lips, she felt a soft, cool breeze caress her face.

'Look over there, I can see daylight,' Naomi cried out.

She was right, and Kirstin could see it too; the soft glow of light. They hurried towards it, the winged creatures silhouetted against the growing daylight.

They reached a stone balcony, decorated with a tracery of gold and overlooking a vast drop. A shaft of sunlight illuminated a waterfall tumbling down to the river far below. Kirstin felt dizzy just looking down at the water and had to grip the balcony to steady herself.

'That's a long way down,' Kirstin said.

Josh looked up, but he couldn't see where the sunlight was coming from.

'It's beautiful,' Naomi whispered, her eyes shining with awe and delight.

'It's also a dead-end,' Josh said. 'Looks like the only way out is back past the giant turkey statues and up the steps.'

'Where the jaguar is?' Kirstin said.

'Or Oddball,' Josh muttered. 'I'm afraid so.'

Naomi groaned. 'Why does everything have to be so difficult?'

Kirstin grabbed Naomi's arm. 'Shush! What was that?'

They stood still and listened. Kirstin was sure she had heard something, but it may have been the rumble of the water-fall playing tricks on her ears.

And then she heard it again.

A low growl.

The jaguar appeared from the gloom surrounding the statues of Quetzalcoatl. It padded slowly towards them, its eyes gleaming in the daylight, its snout red with blood.

Kirstin backed up against the stone balcony. She still had hold of Naomi's arm.

Josh stepped in front of them, between them and the jaguar.

'You're going to have to jump,' he said.

'Oh no,' Kirstin gasped, shaking her

head. 'No way.'

'It's our only option,' Josh said. 'With any luck we'll miss the rocks and the river will be deep enough that we don't hit the riverbed and break our necks.'

'You're not selling this to me,' Kirstin said.

'I don't have to,' Josh replied and pointed at the big cat which was baring its teeth at them and growling again. 'Surely that thing is all the persuasion you need.'

'Mum, it'll be okay,' Naomi said, looking down at the river. 'The water looks deep.'

'How can you tell, all the way up here?'

Naomi threw her head back and groaned. 'I can't believe I'm doing this!'

Before Kirstin had a chance to stop her, Naomi swung her legs over the balcony.

'I love you, Mum!' she shouted, and pushed herself off the edge.

Kirstin watched in a horrified silence as her daughter plummeted into the chasm. Her body grew smaller and smaller until she hit the water and disappeared below the surface.

Kirstin didn't even hear the splash.

She stared, waiting for Naomi to appear from beneath the water's surface.

'She's not coming back up!' Kirstin yelled.

'The current has probably pulled her downriver,' Josh said. 'Your turn now.'

'What?' Kirstin glanced back and saw the jaguar had come much closer.

'He's getting ready to leap at us!'

Josh lifted his hands to fend off the big cat as it sprang for him. The jaguar crashed into Josh, snapping its jaws and snarling. Josh tumbled over the edge of the balcony and plummeted into the chasm.

Kirstin screamed as the jaguar turned its hungry gaze on her. Behind her the waterfall roared.

She had run out of options now.

There was only one way to escape.

Before she knew what she was doing, Kirstin had swung her legs over the balcony and then she was falling too.

The terrifying drop was over in an instant, and yet it seemed to last forever.

Kirstin just had time to remember to take a deep breath before she hit the rushing water, pulled underneath the surface, twisting and tumbling until she didn't know which way was up and which way was down. Naomi had been right, the river was deep. Terrifyingly deep.

The powerful current pulled her downriver. All the daylight had gone and Kirstin was now blind. She had to fight the urge to scream in terror. If she did that, she would lose all her precious air.

And she needed that air, because she had no idea how long it was going to take her to fight her way back to the surface.

The first thing to do was try and regain some control, stop fighting the current and let it carry her wherever it wanted. Kirstin stopped thrashing at the water and curled up into a ball. This made things worse as the powerful current began spinning her around like a football. She straightened out, streamlining herself.

That was better. The river seemed to be straightening out now. Could she find her way to the surface before they hit more rapids? Her lungs were beginning to burn with the need for oxygen. Soon she would be panicking again.

Suddenly water transformed into air and Kirstin opened her mouth and sucked in a greedy lungful of much needed oxygen. For a moment she thought she had risen to the surface of the river, until she realised she was falling.

Another waterfall!

Kirstin plummeted through the darkness, the roar of the falling water surrounding her. Coughing and spluttering, she hit the river's surface and plunged beneath it. This time she didn't manage to hold her breath, and river water gushed into her mouth and tried to force its way into her lungs.

Kirstin coughed and retched. The powerful current pulled at her every which way, as though she was being fought over by a group of giants.

And then again she was ejected from

the water, suspended in mid-air, and falling. Only this time, bright light blinded her. Shadows and sunlight raced across her closed eyelids as she flapped her arms like a bird trying to fly.

This time the fall was mercifully short, and she plunged into the water and then out again like a cork from a bottle. Coughing and gasping for air, Kirstin's hands flailed of their own accord, searching for something to hang onto, something solid.

Miraculously, a hand grabbed hers. Strong arms pulled her from the water and onto the riverbank. Kirstin was rolled onto her side and she coughed up river water, choking and spluttering.

'Mum!'

Kirstin looked up through bleary eyes and saw Naomi running towards her.

'Naomi?'

Before she had a chance to say anything else, Kirstin was swallowed in Naomi's embrace.

The two of them hugged and cried and hugged some more. When Kirstin had stopped spluttering and coughing, she was able to sit up and take a look at her surroundings. They were back outside again. The sun shone from a clear blue sky, the powerful river sparkling in the light as it tumbled downhill.

A group of villagers crowded on the riverbank, chattering excitedly.

'They rescued us both,' Naomi said. 'They saw us and pulled us out of the water.'

'But where's Josh?' Kirstin said, gazing up at the waterfall just yards away from where they sat.

He should have been here. Josh fell off the balcony before Kirstin. Why wasn't he here?

The mountain range towered over them, the water pouring from a rocky opening in the side of the cliff face. What had happened to him? Had Kirstin lost Josh forever?

With a strangled yell, Josh hurtled from the cave like a bullet from a gun and fell, arms flailing, to the rushing water below. The villagers erupted in cheers of joy and laughter as he splashed into the river, disappearing below the surface. Moments later he resurfaced. Two of the men waded out and grabbed him and hauled him onto dry ground.

Josh lay face down and coughed and spluttered.

Kirstin grinned.

They were alive.

21

Kirstin, Naomi and Josh were led back to a village by their rescuers. Turned out they were a day's hike further up the mountain than where they had found the cave entrance to the Lost City behind the waterfall. Kirstin couldn't work out how that could be possible, as they had jumped into the river from the balcony in the underground temple, and yet here they were, higher than where they had first begun their journey. The route through the cave system, through the village and then the Lost City had to have been ascending even though much of the time they had seemed to be descending.

Kirstin decided not to think about it anymore. There was so much she didn't understand about the Lost City, about the underground world they had found with its own ecosystem, and many other things too. And she had the distinct feeling she never would know.

Josh had narrowly escaped with his life. When the jaguar had pounced at Josh and knocked him over the balcony he had been grabbed by the current and taken downriver.

At one point the current had pulled him against the side of the riverbed where he had managed to grab hold of a rocky outcrop. He had hung on for several moments while he gulped down some air and then let go again.

Of the three of them, Josh had suffered the worst with a black eye and some bruising to his chest and arms.

They were looked after by the villagers and then two days later headed back to the village where they had hired the boat.

Here they were able to hitch a ride to the nearest town, where they booked into a hotel and got themselves cleaned up and rested and slept through the night.

The following morning they met for breakfast.

Naomi had the drawstring bag with her, containing the catapult and the three small rocks given to her by Minika. She laid everything out on the breakfast table and looked at it sadly.

'You wish you could go back, don't you?' Kirstin said, taking her daughter's hand.

'Sort of,' Naomi said. 'I mean, mostly I just want to go home, but I'm sad that I won't see Minika again, or Edwin and Iliana.'

'I hope the old man made it back to the village alright,' Josh said. 'I hated leaving him in that forest.'

'Me too,' Kirstin said. In fact, she'd thought of little else once they had reached the safety of the town. If only she could find some way of getting in contact with the village, just to put her mind at rest that Edwin was alive and well.

'Well, he was a tough old guy,' Josh said. 'I'm betting he's back now, glad to have some peace and quiet again.'

'I hope so,' Naomi said.

'The swelling is starting to go down,' Kirstin said, looking at Josh's face.

The bruising around his eyes had

turned yellow, but his left eye which had swollen shut was starting to open up again.

'Yeah, but I'll never be the beauty that I was before.'

'I think it's an improvement,' Naomi said and giggled, ducking as she avoided the wadded up napkin he threw at her.

'What are you going to do now?' Kirstin said.

Josh thought for a moment. 'Well, I guess the first thing will be to make an insurance claim on Janice, and then buy myself a new plane.'

'What will you call your new one?' Kirstin said.

Josh shrugged. 'Not sure. To be honest, I'm not even that convinced I want to go back to ferrying tourists around in the air. Everything feels different now.'

Kirstin had a sudden urge to grab Josh's hand and tell him to come back to England with her. They could marry, and he could be the father to Naomi that she had never had, but so desperately needed.

And was Josh thinking the same thing? The space between them suddenly seemed charged with electricity. The way he held her in his gaze, the expression on his bruised face.

'I don't know, though,' he said, looking away and breaking the spell. 'What else am I going to do with my life? Flying tourists over the rainforest is pretty much all I'm good for now.'

Kirstin wanted to tell him that wasn't true, that he shouldn't hold himself back, that the way Julia had treated him in their marriage wasn't a reflection of who he truly was. But the words stuck in her chest, and all she could do was look helplessly at him.

'Honestly, you two!' Naomi snapped. 'Why can't you both see that you're perfect for each other?'

Josh cast Naomi a look that said lots, but he didn't speak. Instead, he climbed to his feet.

'I'm going to get my stuff together and check out. I think it's probably best if we just say goodbye here, right now.'

Kirstin's chest seemed to be collapsing in on itself. There was so much she wanted to say.

'Mum!' Naomi said. 'Don't let him go!'

Kirstin glanced at her daughter and then looked back at Josh. Kirstin wished she had Naomi's certainty, that if she told Josh to stay he would. And yet, the look on his face. So much seemed to have changed since they held hands in the underground village. Back there had been magical, and the future had seemed full of possibilities. But now, headed back to the real world?

Charles and Julia might be gone, but it seemed their shadows still loomed large.

'I think Mr Hanson needs to make up his own mind about staying or going,' Kirstin said.

Naomi rounded on Josh. 'Don't go, stay with us, come back to England.'

Josh shook his head sadly. 'I think it's better this way.'

'Thank you, Mr Hanson, for looking after us,' Kirstin said.

Josh nodded and then turned, and walked out of the dining room.

'That's it?' Naomi hissed. 'You're just going to let him leave?'

'What else am I supposed to do?' Kirstin said.

'Go after him, tell him how you feel about him!'

Kirstin shook her head, sadly. 'No, I can't do that.'

'Why not? He's obviously crazy about you, and you feel the same way about him.'

'It's . . . it's more complicated than that.'

Naomi groaned and flung herself back into her chair. 'You're hopeless, both of you!'

Kirstin stood up. 'Come on, we need to get our things together and leave. We have a flight to catch back to England.'

They climbed the narrow stairs up to their room. Kirstin couldn't stop thinking about what Naomi had said. Maybe she was right, and they were crazy about each other. Kirstin's heart ached heavily at the thought of not seeing Josh again.

But did he feel the same way?

She paused outside their room. Josh's room was directly opposite.

Naomi looked at her. 'Mum?'

Kirstin sighed. 'Do you really think he might like me?'

'Oh, Mum!' Naomi gave Kirstin an exasperated look. 'He's completely mad about you!'

Could Naomi be right? Could Josh have feelings for Kirstin? Especially after all the hurt Julia had caused him. Josh had even said he was never having a relationship again, that he would never allow himself to feel love for someone else. Charles and Julia had done immense damage in both of their lives, but did it have to stay that way?

And even if Naomi was wrong about Josh's feelings, surely it was still worth taking a chance?

Naomi took Kirstin's hand in hers. 'Mum?'

Kirstin barely heard her daughter. For a moment she was back in Edwin's village, standing with Josh and holding hands. Promising each other that they would take things easy, slowly. Acknowledging the possibility that they could heal from old wounds.

That they could do it together.

Kirstin gave Naomi the room key. 'You go in and start packing. I'm going to pay Josh a visit.'

Naomi punched the air. 'Yes!'

Kirstin waited until Naomi had entered their room and closed the door. Taking a deep breath and gathering her courage, Kirstin knocked on Josh's door.

Silence. Surely he couldn't have left already?

Kirstin knocked again and waited.

Nothing. It sounded as though the room was empty. Had Josh left by a back exit, perhaps? Had he been so desperate to not see Kirstin again? Maybe she had judged Josh wrong, and he had no feelings towards her. Just the opposite perhaps, and he had felt the urge to leave without risking seeing her anymore.

Kirstin took a deep, slightly shaky breath. This was it, then. She would never see Josh again. Kirstin turned her back on his hotel room door.

And froze as she heard a bump from within his room. Like someone had dropped something.

He was there!

What was he doing? Ignoring her?

Kirstin's insides filled with a sudden anger and indignation. How dare he ignore her? Maybe he was damaged from his relationship with Julia, and maybe he had sworn never to fall in love again, but that didn't mean he should cower in his room like a terrified teenage boy.

Kirstin spun around, raised her fist and hammered on the door. 'Josh! You let me in right now!'

She grabbed the door handle and twisted it.

The door was unlocked.

Swinging the door open, Kirstin stepped inside and immediately pulled up short with a cry of surprise.

Oddball had his arm around Josh's neck, strangling him. Josh pulled at Oddball's arm as he choked, his face turning purple, his eyes bulging with panic. He kicked out, trying to yank himself free of Oddball's grip, but the giant was just too strong.

Picking up a lamp off a cabinet, Kirstin screamed and ran for Oddball, raising the lamp high and ready to smash it on his head. The lamp flew from her hand, pulled by the electric wire still plugged into the wall socket, and fell to the floor.

Kirstin kicked Oddball in the shin and grabbed at his arm, trying to release the grip on Josh's neck. She might as well have been attacking a massive boulder. With his free hand, Oddball shoved Kirstin out of the way and she tumbled to the floor.

The lamp she had dropped lay on the wooden floor boards, only inches from her nose.

Scrabbling to her feet, Kirstin picked up the lamp again and yanked hard, pulling the electric cable from the base. With the lamp free of its tether, Kirstin swung it with all her strength and smashed it over the top of Oddball's skull.

The giant let go of Josh, who collapsed to the floor coughing and spluttering. Ignoring him, Oddball turned his attention to Kirstin. The full force of his dark eyes seemed to pin her down, making her incapable of any rational thought. Her legs turned to jelly as he towered over her.

Oddball gripped Kirstin by the shoulders and lifted her like she was a doll. Silently he threw her across the room. The walls, the ceiling, the floor, all of it became a blur. Kirstin hit the bed on her side and then rolled off it. The impact had knocked the breath out of her and she lay, stunned, unable to move.

Oddball's heavy footfall approached.

Could nobody else in the hotel hear what was going on? Wouldn't someone come and help them?

Massive hands lifted Kirstin off the floor. She caught a glimpse of Josh, who was trying to get to his feet but still coughing helplessly. Oddball lifted Kirstin high and carried her over to the room's window.

Kirstin started kicking and struggling. They were on the first floor. If Oddball threw her from the window, she would almost certainly die.

Oddball stopped. Josh, still on the floor, had grabbed the giant's ankle.

'Leave her alone!' Josh croaked.

The hotel door opened. 'Mum!'

Oddball kicked Josh in the side, freeing himself of his hold on his leg. He turned back to the window. Kirstin had no strength left to fight. Oddball lifted her high.

And dropped her.

Kirstin landed with a bone jarring thump on the floor, knocking the breath from her lungs. Oddball stood over her, a hand clapped to the back of his neck and a puzzled expression on his face. He turned around.

Naomi stood in the doorway, her catapult held out at arm's length and ready to fire.

'Take this, you big freak!'

She let go of the cord and the hard, pointed rock smacked Oddball right in the centre of his forehead. Stunned, the giant staggered back and dropped to the floor on his bottom. He touched his forehead and his fingertips came away bloody.

Oddball's face contorted in fury as he stared at the scarlet blood.

'Naomi, run!' Kirstin screamed.

Naomi turned and fled.

Oddball climbed to his feet and headed for the open door. Josh crashed into him in a rugby tackle and they both hit the floor with a sickening smack. Oddball threw Josh off like he was a child and stood up.

Josh lay on the floor, a fit of coughing convulsing through him. Oddball raised a foot, ready to kick the helpless man.

'Leave him alone!' Kirstin yelled as she stood up.

Oddball paused and turned to look at her.

His dark eyes narrowed down to tiny little slits.

And it suddenly seemed to Kirstin that all his rage was focused on her.

Screwing his hands into fists, the giant ran for her as his lips peeled back in a furious snarl.

With nowhere to go, Kirstin dived for the floor, scrambling to crawl under the bed. She felt Oddball's foot catch her ankle. The giant hurtled forward and hit the room's window. With a smash of glass, he fell through and down to the street below.

Kirstin scrambled to her feet and looked out of the broken window.

Oddball lay on his back on the ground, his limbs splayed out and completely still.

Josh and Naomi joined her. They watched as a crowd began gathering around the body.

Josh gently massaged his neck.

Kirstin turned and wrapped her arms around both Josh and Naomi.

And she wasn't letting go of either of them.

22

The church bells rang out loud and clear from the village church. Kirstin's father held out a hand, and she took it as she climbed out of the wedding car. The day was pleasantly warm, the sky a deep, beautiful blue.

'You look lovely,' he said.

'Thank you,' Kirstin replied, and smiled.

Some of the locals had gathered to watch. Kirstin glanced over at them.

'Where's Naomi?' She was supposed to be here, waiting with her grandfather.

'She's waiting at the church, she has a surprise for you.'

Intrigued, Kirstin took her father's arm, and they walked down the path through the churchyard to the open church doors.

They paused. From inside, Kirstin could hear the dying notes of the organ. Any moment now and the organist would start up the wedding march. Kirstin's stomach fluttered with excitement and nerves.

It seemed like no time at all had passed since she last stood outside a church (well, a cathedral last time) about to enter and be married. Back then it hadn't ended so well, but Kirstin knew today would be different.

Her father smiled. 'There's Naomi, look. Escorting a very special surprise wedding guest to you.'

Kirstin's eyes still hadn't properly adjusted from the bright sunshine to the church's interior, but she could see Naomi standing up and helping someone beside her to their feet. Together they walked down the aisle towards the front of the church where Kirstin and her father waited.

Who was this mysterious surprise guest?

Wait . . . was that . . . Edwin?

As he drew nearer, Edwin smiled and waved. He looked very handsome in his suit, but older too than Kirstin remembered. He threw his arms around her and they hugged.

'I can't believe it!' Kirstin said, stepping back. 'Have you really come all this way for the wedding?'

Edwin nodded, his eyes shining. 'After seeing you and Naomi, I realised how much of family life I had missed by not being here these last few decades. That I never got to see my great niece growing up.' He looped his arm through Kirstin's. 'Or my great, great niece.' And he looped his other arm around Naomi's.

'Is Iliana here?' Kirstin said.

Edwin nodded. 'She is in the church and wants to say hello once you are married. Now, I must go and join her as I think I am holding up the wedding procession.'

Kirstin gripped his hand. 'Join us, escort me down the aisle with Dad and Naomi.'

The old man hesitated.

'Please,' Kirstin said. 'It would mean so much to me, to have you, Walter's brother, walking me down the aisle.'

'Go on, Edwin, please do!' Naomi

said, beaming at the old man.

Edwin smiled and nodded. 'It would be my pleasure.'

The church organ began playing the wedding march.

Through the open doors, Kirstin could see Josh standing at the front.

Waiting for his bride.

Waiting for Kirstin.

★　★　★

'Oh, it was so beautiful!'

Jacqui threw her arms around Kirstin's neck and began sobbing.

Kirstin giggled and embraced her sister. 'Don't be silly, come on, don't cry.'

'I can't help it,' Jacqui sobbed, her voice muffled in Kirstin's head dress. 'You look so beautiful, and the church service was beautiful, and it's all so amazing.'

Kirstin looked over Jacqui's head at David, who simply raised his eyebrows and gave Kirstin an uncomfortable smile. Behind him snaked the line of wedding guests still waiting to greet the bride and groom.

Kirstin had a slightly uncomfortable feeling of deja vu. Hadn't this been exactly what had happened in Italy when she had married Charles?

As if to reinforce that thought, Jacqui suddenly pulled away from Kirstin and wiped at her red and puffy eyes with the heel of her hand. Stabbing a finger in Josh's chest, Jacqui said, 'Now you make sure you look after her, or you'll have me to answer to.'

Josh, looking so very handsome in his suit, held up his hands in surrender. 'I promise, I promise!'

'You'd better,' Jacqui said, before giving Kirstin another hug. 'Come on, David, you're holding up the wedding line.'

David looked down at his feet as he muttered something.

Kirstin laughed out loud. If only they realised they were replaying the wedding day in Italy.

And then she stopped laughing, remembering Julia had been the next guest in the line. Remembering that handshake between Charles and Julia that went on just a touch too long.

And then remembering how she found them both in the bridal suite. If only she had realised at the time that it had all been part of a plot against her.

Kirstin still thought about Julia sometimes. Her body had not been found at the temple, and Kirstin wondered if she had managed to escape with Oddball. But if that was the case, they had parted ways soon after.

Kirstin wondered if she would ever see Julia again.

'Are you okay?' Josh whispered in her ear. 'You look like you've just seen a ghost.'

'In a way, I think I have,' Kirstin said, thoughtfully.

Josh looked quizzically at her, but Kirstin smiled and shook her head. It didn't matter anymore. Everything had turned out for the best, because if Charles and Julia hadn't schemed and acted the way they did then Kirstin might never have met Josh.

She turned back to the never ending line of wedding guests.

The rest of the day passed in a flurry of food, (four courses), almost endlessly flowing rivers of alcohol (champagne and wine), wedding cake, (three tiers) and speeches.

'As I am sure many of you already know, my eldest daughter has a passion for looking for things,' Kirstin's father said in his speech. 'Ancient things, not just the TV remote stuffed down the back of the settee, or anything like that. No, my daughter enjoys looking for ancient, long lost cities. Last year she set off on the adventure of a lifetime, determined to find the Lost City of . . . oh hang on, what's it called again, Josh?'

'Did you put him up to this?' Josh muttered to Kirstin.

She giggled. 'Go on, answer my dad, everybody's waiting.'

Josh cleared his throat as the hall full of wedding guests waited for him to speak. 'It's called the Lost City of Quilt . . .

Qualsa . . . Quetcal . . . oh, I don't know how to say it!'

The guests burst into laughter.

'The Lost City of Quetzalcoatl,' Kirstin's father said, laughing too. 'Yes, she went looking for a lost city, but instead she returned having found something far more important; love.'

A murmur of approval rippled through the wedding guests.

'But Kirstin didn't just find romantic love. Besides finding a husband for herself, she found a father for Naomi, and an uncle and aunt for myself.'

Edwin and Iliana clasped hands at their table and beamed with pleasure.

'And I couldn't be happier, or more proud.'

Kirstin looked up at her father, and he gazed back at her.

He raised his glass. The wedding guests stood up and raised their glasses too.

'Please stand as we toast the bride and groom. May your love for each other fly high and far above the clouds and in the

302

sunshine, and may you never come back down to earth. To the bride and groom!'

★ ★ ★

After that unsettling moment earlier in the day when Kirstin had been reminded of her previous wedding day in Italy, Kirstin didn't think about Julia and Charles again until later at the evening reception. Weary but happy, Kirstin felt ready to leave for their honeymoon. Except, Josh had kept the honeymoon a closely guarded secret. And now that she thought about it, she couldn't see her new husband anywhere.

'Have you seen Josh?' she said to her dad. 'I can't find him.'

'No, I'm sorry I haven't,' her father said.

Kirstin's parents were sat with Edwin and Iliana and they were all deep in conversation.

Looking around the hall, Kirstin realised she hadn't seen Naomi for a little while either. Stirrings of unease grew in

Kirstin's stomach as she inadvertently thought back once more to her wedding day in Venice.

Don't be silly, she scalded herself. Nothing like that is going to happen today.

But still, as if her disastrous wedding to Charles was destined to repeat itself, Kirstin found herself heading towards her room. She climbed the hotel stairs. Her feet ached in her wedding shoes and she paused to slip them off.

Hadn't this been the way it happened last time?

Kirstin padded barefoot down the wide hall. She paused outside her room and listened, waiting for the sound of Julia's giggle.

Stop it! Kirstin thought. Julia isn't here, nor Charles.

A wave of cold fear washed over Kirstin as she heard a giggle from her room after all.

How could this be happening again?

Kirstin threw open the door.

Josh and Naomi, sitting cross-legged

on the floor, looked up at Kirstin.

'Uh-oh, she found us,' Josh said, grinning, and they both fell into another helpless fit of giggling.

'What's going on?' Kirstin asked, weakly.

A map had been spread out across the floor. Naomi jumped to her feet and stepped over it. She ran to her mum and took her hand.

'It's time!' she called to Josh. 'Let's go downstairs.'

Giggling again, Naomi and Josh guided Kirstin back downstairs to the reception where the guests were mingling and chatting.

'Could I have everybody's attention, please?' Naomi shouted. 'The bride and groom are about to depart. Please could you all proceed outside to see them off on their next adventure?'

Kirstin watched, puzzled, as the guests slowly fled out of the hotel and gathered in the grounds.

'What's going on?' she said again. It seemed she couldn't think of anything else to say.

Josh took her hand. 'You'll see.'

Josh and Naomi led Kirstin outside.

There, parked in the hotel grounds, was a light aircraft.

'Wait, what? I don't understand.'

'It's Janice, Mark Two,' Naomi said, laughing.

'Actually no,' Josh said.'This plane is a boy, so I couldn't call him Janice. His name is Walter.'

Kirstin flung her arms around Josh and kissed him and held him tight. All the guests began clapping.

'Come on, we need to get up in the air,' Josh said.

Kirstin touched foreheads with Josh. 'But where are we going?'

'You'll see!'

'You are being very mysterious, Mr Hanson.'

'But I thought Mrs Hanson enjoyed mysteries.'

'Oh I do, I do.'

And they kissed again.

Hurried goodbyes were said, along with hugs and tears.

Kirstin held on to Naomi for as long as she could.

'Mum, you've got to go,' Naomi said.

'I know, I know,' Kirstin replied, her voice thick with emotion. There seemed to be so much more to say to her daughter, this amazing young woman who had seen through Charles from the beginning and who had stood by her and been so brave. And yet, Kirstin couldn't find the words.

When she pulled back and looked into Naomi's eyes, Kirstin realised there was nothing to say after all. That Naomi understood.

Kirstin and Josh ran to the Cessna and Josh helped Kirstin climb inside. He clambered into the cockpit too and started the engine. The propellers whirred into life.

They both turned and waved at the wedding guests.

'So, Mr Hanson, just where are we going?'

'Where do you want to go? North? South? Or will anywhere on the compass do?'

'Stop teasing me!' Kirstin punched her husband lightly on the arm. 'I saw that map you and Naomi were looking at. You already know where we are going.'

Josh began taxiing the plane away from the guests.

'Will this thing even get off the ground?' Kirstin said.

'Just you watch,' Josh said.

The engine's note picked up and then they were magically leaving the ground. Kirstin whooped with joy as they climbed into the sky. Josh banked the plane and Kirstin saw her family and friends on the ground, waving up at them.

Kirstin waved back, laughing.

She turned back to Josh as he levelled the aircraft out. Ahead of them the blue sky stretched into infinity.

'Alright mister, no more messing about, where are we going?'

'Look on the back seat,' Josh said.

Kirstin swivelled around and saw a notebook lying on the back seat of the plane. She picked it up and turned forward again as she opened it up.

'This is one of Walter's notebooks!'

'Yeah, Naomi and your dad have been showing them to me. And we found mention of another lost city. One that even your amazing grandfather never managed to find.'

'And that's where we are going?'

Josh grinned. 'Well, if we can find it, yeah.'

Kirstin leaned over and kissed Josh. 'I love you.'

'Good, because I love you too.'

Kirstin settled herself into her seat and gazed at the view.

A view filled with possibilities and adventure.

We do hope that you have enjoyed reading this large print book.

Did you know that all of our titles are available for purchase?

We publish a wide range of high quality large print books including:
Romances, Mysteries, Classics
General Fiction
Non Fiction and Westerns

Special interest titles available in large print are:
The Little Oxford Dictionary
Music Book, Song Book
Hymn Book, Service Book

Also available from us courtesy of Oxford University Press:
Young Readers' Dictionary
(large print edition)
Young Readers' Thesaurus
(large print edition)

For further information or a free brochure, please contact us at:
Ulverscroft Large Print Books Ltd.,
The Green, Bradgate Road, Anstey,
Leicester, LE7 7FU, England.
Tel: (00 44) 0116 236 4325
Fax: (00 44) 0116 234 0205

Other titles in the
Linford Romance Library:

UPSTAIRS, DOWNSTAIRS

Alice Elliott

Rumours are flying around the servants' quarters at Brackenfold Hall. Items are going missing, and nobody knows who to trust anymore. Fingers start pointing at Bess, the sullen new scullery maid — but housemaid Sally Halfpenny feels sure she isn't to blame. Sally vows to uncover the true identity of the thief. Meanwhile, a fever has hit the whole village, and she fears for the safety of her parents. Not to mention the anguish of her unrequited love for footman James Armstrong . . .

WHEN A WOMAN LOVES

Denise Robins

Sandra was the kind of girl men found irresistible. Hugh Lancaster, the famous artist for whom she posed, deserted his wife and was driven to suicide. Michael Hunt, the only man she ever loved, married her – but risked ruining both their lives because of her past. Then there was Victor Bentley, the debauched playboy, whose designs on her threatened to deepen the tragedy . . .

A DEBT FOR ROSALIE

Anne Stenhouse

Rosalie Garden arrives at Malding-ton House, an upmarket guest house, to work as a chef and earn enough to repay her father who bailed her out after her ex brought down her catering business. David Logie is the house's owner, and son of the pro-prietor Agnes. Still mourning the early death of his wife, David wants to sell his inheritance. Together with Agnes, Rosalie works hard to frus-trate David's plans – and bring him to realise that he can love again . . .